One touch w

Marley's tank top had ridden up, and Caleb found himself touching bare skin. Bare, warm skin, so soft that he hissed in a breath.

"I..." Marley's voice drifted and her mouth fell open when she saw the desire in his eyes.

He could do nothing to hide his swift response. Her flesh felt like heaven, and her sweet scent was far too intoxicating. Before he could stop himself, he moved his hand over her hip in a fleeting caress. An unsteady breath slid out of her throat.

Insanity. This was freaking insanity, and he was helpless to stop it. He'd been watching Marley Kincaid for seven days, watching and yearning and fighting the arousal he knew he shouldn't be feeling.

But he couldn't fight it now. Not when she was this close.

Screw it. Kissing her was wrong on so many levels, but at this point, he didn't care. He wanted her so badly his bones ached.

So he took her...

Blaze™

Dear Reader,

I'm thrilled about my second release from Harlequin Blaze. This book started out as a mere inkling of an idea—*what if you were being watched...and you didn't know it?* Oh, and the guy watching you just happened to be a sexy cop.

I've posed this question to many of my friends. The consensus seems to be that, as much as we love the bad boy, there's something overwhelmingly appealing about a man with authority who's on the *right* side of the law. I hope you enjoy Caleb and Marley's story. I had a lot of fun writing it and painting my rugged hero as a good guy...who's bad in all the right places!

Keep your curtains closed....

Elle

Elle Kennedy

WITNESS SEDUCTION

TORONTO NEW YORK LONDON
AMSTERDAM PARIS SYDNEY HAMBURG
STOCKHOLM ATHENS TOKYO MILAN MADRID
PRAGUE WARSAW BUDAPEST AUCKLAND

Recycling programs
for this product may
not exist in your area.

ISBN-13: 978-0-373-79641-0

WITNESS SEDUCTION

ABOUT THE AUTHOR

Elle Kennedy grew up in the suburbs of Toronto, Ontario, and holds a B.A. in English from York University. From an early age, she knew she wanted to be a writer, and actively began pursuing that dream when she was only a teenager. When she's not writing, she's reading. And when she's not reading, she's making music with her drummer boyfriend, oil painting or indulging her love for board games.

Elle loves to hear from her readers. Visit her at her website www.ellekennedy.com to send her a note.

Books by Elle Kennedy

HARLEQUIN BLAZE
458—BODY CHECK

SILHOUETTE ROMANTIC SUSPENSE
1574—SILENT WATCH
1634—HER PRIVATE AVENGER

To get the inside scoop on Harlequin Blaze and its talented writers, be sure to check out blazeauthors.com.

Don't miss any of our special offers. Write to us at the following address for information on our newest releases.

Harlequin Reader Service
U.S.: 3010 Walden Ave., P.O. Box 1325, Buffalo, NY 14269
Canadian: P.O. Box 609, Fort Erie, Ont. L2A 5X3

For Amanda

1

"OKAY, HOW ABOUT THIS—you're walking down the street and suddenly you bump into a tall, dark and handsome stranger who sweeps you off your feet, looks deep into your eyes and says, 'I have never seen such exquisite beauty. Have coffee with me, my mysterious maiden.' Would you go out with him?"

Marley Kincaid burst into laughter, nearly spilling her coffee all over the oak work island in the middle of her kitchen. She set down the mug and grinned at her best friend. "'My mysterious maiden'?" she echoed. "Uh, yeah, I'm not sure I could go out with any man who called me that."

Gwen Shaffer rolled her eyes. "Okay, pretend he didn't say that. He's just a drop-dead gorgeous guy who wants to buy you a cup of coffee. Would you go?"

"I don't know. Maybe." Marley sighed. "Why are you so eager to get me dating again?"

Gwen had raised the subject the second she'd walked into the house nearly an hour ago, and Marley was growing tired of it. She didn't usually mind when Gwen popped in on her day off to chat over coffee, but this conversation was beginning to annoy her. Somehow it had gone from Gwen trying to convince her to go on a blind date to what-if scenarios that made no sense. She knew her friend meant well, but what was the point in talking about all the possible ways she might meet a man?

"Because you've barely left this house in months," Gwen replied. "I want to see you having fun again. All you do is paint and put up wallpaper and—"

"I'm renovating," Marley interrupted. "And I'm enjoying it."

"You're hiding from the world, and you know it." Gwen's tone softened. "Look, I understand, hon. That bastard is still on the run. If it were me, I'd be worried, too. I mean, what if he shows up here pleading for help or something?"

Marley's entire body tensed. She swallowed hard, turning her head so she was spared the familiar flicker of sympathy in her friend's dark-green eyes. She hated it when Gwen brought up Patrick. Hated being reminded of the disastrous relationship that had ended in a train wreck she hadn't seen coming.

Eight months ago, she'd been on top of the world. Working at a job she loved, buying her first home, falling in love.

Well, she still had the job and the house, but the man she loved? Turned out he hadn't been all that worthy of her undying affection.

She'd met Patrick at the hospital, where he'd been recovering from a nasty stab wound to his side. Mugged on his way home from work, or so she'd believed at the time. She'd been assigned to his room, and it hadn't taken long for Patrick's easygoing charm to lure her in.

They went on their first date the night he got discharged from the hospital and, three weeks later, he practically moved into her house. Four months after that, they were engaged.

It'd lasted five months. Five months of great sex and laughter and that wonderful feeling of falling in love with a handsome, attentive man. He'd wrapped her in a protective bubble and made her believe anything was possible. Patrick had been good at that, playing make-believe. So good that when the cops had come knocking on her door, she'd actually defended him.

She still remembered the disbelief on those police officers' faces when she'd finally realized the truth. That her fiancé was not a freelance web designer, but a drug distributor. Not to mention the prime suspect in the fatal shooting of a federal agent.

God, what a fool she'd been.

"He won't show up," she said darkly. "He's probably lying on a beach in Mexico, laughing at the law-enforcement officers who couldn't catch him."

Fortunately, Patrick hadn't tried contacting her since he'd fled three months before, and good riddance. She never wanted to see that man again, and for the past few months she'd gone to great lengths to permanently erase him from her life. Burned his clothes in the backyard, flushed his engagement ring down the toilet.

Too bad none of that had succeeded in actually exorcising him from her mind.

"I'm not too happy with the cops, either," Gwen said with a frown. "I still can't believe they thought you were involved."

Marley's lips tightened. "Detective Hernandez couldn't accept that I was so naive. How could I not know my fiancé was a criminal?"

"You weren't naive. Patrick was just a good liar."

"Yeah, he was." Marley picked up her mug, along with Gwen's empty one, and set them both in the sink. "At least the police are finally leaving me alone. I only hope it stays that way. Now, can we please stop talking about Patrick?"

Gwen's face brightened. "Okay. Can we talk about Nick's friend then?"

Marley suppressed a groan. "I told you, I'm not interested."

"I'm not suggesting you marry the guy. It's just a date. One measly little date. You said you were ready to date again."

"No, I said I might be." She blew a stray strand of hair off her forehead. "But a blind date isn't the way I want to go about it, okay? I'm not having dinner with a complete stranger. It's too forced, too…intimate."

"Then we'll make it a double date."

"No." Without looking at Gwen, she swallowed back the bitterness sticking to her throat and added, "I can't agree to go out with a stranger. I can't do it, Gwen. Not now, anyway."

"Fine, but the subject's not closed, you know. We'll talk about it later." Gwen hopped off the stool, her brown curls bouncing on her shoulders, and reached for the black leather purse she'd set on the counter. "I have to run. I'm meeting Nick for lunch."

Marley followed her friend out of the kitchen, her bare feet slapping against the weathered hardwood floor. They reached the front hall, sidestepping the stack of two-by-fours obstructing the way. Marley's younger brother, Sam, had promised to extend the coat closet by a couple feet, so last weekend he'd come over and hacked away at the wall. Then he'd gotten a phone call and taken off to handle a work emergency. He hadn't been back since, and Marley was now left with a gaping hole in the floor and all the supplies he'd brought into her hallway.

She didn't mind, though. Sam was busy working at their dad's construction company, and it made her happy he was doing well. Her brother had always been irresponsible and scatterbrained growing up. It was nice seeing him act like an adult, even if it did mean he'd left his sister in the lurch.

Gwen paused on the front porch. "Want to come to lunch with us?" she offered.

"Thanks, but I'll pass." Marley was so not in the mood to watch Gwen make googly eyes at her long-time boyfriend. The two of them still acted as if they were in the mushy newlywed stage when in fact they'd been together for years.

Her friend looked suspicious. "How are you planning to spend the rest of your day off?"

"Cleaning out the eaves," she said, fighting back a smile.

Gwen blew out a frustrated breath. "You're incorrigible."

Marley's smile reached the surface. "Yeah, but you love me anyway."

"Can't argue that. All right, I'll see you at the hospital tomorrow." Gwen leaned in to give her a quick side hug, then bounded down the porch steps toward the shiny black Jeep parked behind the red Mazda convertible Marley had owned since she was eighteen years old.

Marley waved at her friend, watched Gwen speed away, then walked back inside. Alone, she let out a heavy sigh. Talking about Patrick always brought this awful feeling to her stomach. A cross between sorrow and bitterness, with a hefty dose of anger thrown into the mix. Everyone in her life kept pushing her to forget about him—Gwen, their friends from the hospital, her dad, her brother.

None of them seemed to get it. They didn't understand how badly Patrick had hurt her. Not only that, but he'd taken a skewer to her judgment and punched so many holes in it she wasn't sure she could ever trust her instincts again.

What kind of woman fell in love with a murderer? How could she have been so blind to Patrick's deception? She knew she wasn't the first and wouldn't be the last woman to be duped by a man. Heck, she'd once watched an entire documentary about serial killers and how they skillfully deceived their loved ones.

But that didn't make this situation any better. She still felt like a fool. She'd completely fallen for Patrick's lies and she hated how easily he'd conned her. He'd even convinced her to open a joint savings account, saying they'd need one anyway when they were married. Good thing she hadn't gotten around to depositing anything into it, but it still irked—especially since she couldn't close the damn thing because the cops had frozen it.

And sure, maybe she was hiding from the world, just a little, but the renovations on her house helped keep her mind off her fugitive ex-fiancé. Besides, she really was enjoying the work.

Her place was nestled in a neighborhood of quaint Victorians and leafy elm trees at the end of the cul-de-sac. Two stories high, it was painted pale cream and in desperate need of new shutters. But she loved the old place. She planned on tackling the exterior after the inside was all spruced up.

Heading to the laundry room, she grabbed all the cleaning supplies she needed. She slipped her feet into a pair of white sneakers, then hauled her bucket of supplies out to the side of the house, where the wooden ladder she'd set up earlier leaned against the slate-green roof.

Fine, so maybe cleaning out eaves wasn't the most exciting thing to do on one's day off, but it needed to be done. And who knew, maybe one of Gwen's what-if scenarios would come true.

A tall, dark and handsome stranger approaches the house. "My mysterious maiden," he says. "Your beauty overwhelms me. Let me clean your rain gutters."

Marley smothered a laugh. Rolling her eyes, she snapped a pair of rubber gloves onto her hands and climbed the first rung of the ladder.

"*This* maiden needs no man to take care of her," she murmured to herself with a grin.

CALEB FORD LEANED BACK in the plush swivel chair and wondered when exactly he'd become a voyeur. His job had forced him to sit through many a stakeout but somehow this one seemed…wrong.

Arousing as hell…but damn it, *wrong*.

He'd been a DEA agent for ten years, had put dozens of criminals behind bars, gotten shot twice in his career—and yet this one little stakeout was killing him. It should've been easy, a wait-and-grab he could've done in his sleep. The location was perfect, the electronic equipment was sweet, and his target, despite the irregular hours she worked, didn't leave the house much.

Yep, in theory, this stakeout should've been a piece of cake.

But none of his theories had taken into consideration the powerful allure of Marley Kincaid.

Caleb shifted in the chair, hoping to ease the ache in his groin. A sip of the cold soda sitting on the desk in front of him helped cool his throat, but did nothing to snuff out the fire in his lower body.

A quick glance at the screens displaying Marley's front and back doors showed no movement. Not that he had to be so vigilant; the motion detectors they'd set up caused the monitors to release a loud buzz every time anyone walked by them. There was plenty of movement at the side of the house, however.

Marley was up on a ladder, wearing faded cut-off shorts, a red tank top and yellow rubber gloves, and she was cleaning out the eaves using a long brush. Wet leaves and mud went sailing down to the grass ten feet below, remnants of last night's thunderstorm.

Damn, she was cute up there on the ladder, her blond ponytail swishing back and forth as she worked. When he'd taken the case, he'd seen pictures of Marley, sure, but seeing her in person was a different story altogether. It had been a week since he'd hunkered down next door to her, and already he'd memorized every detail of her face—her golden-brown eyes set over a pair of unbelievably high cheekbones, her cute up-turned nose, her full sensual lips. God, those lips. She had a mouth made for sin. Not to mention a body that could cause a man to forget his own name.

For seven days now he'd wondered what she looked like naked. But they only had clearance to install cameras outside the house. And she always closed her drapes when she undressed, forcing his imagination to run wild as he stared at her enticing silhouette removing various undergarments.

His cell phone began to ring, a much-needed distraction from the woman next door.

Sighing, he snatched the phone from its perch near the computer keyboard and pressed the talk button. "Ford," he said. His voice came out hoarse, and he had to clear his throat before speaking again.

"I'm at the Starbucks around the corner," came AJ Callaghan's southern drawl. "Want some coffee?"

Caleb tore his gaze away from the monitor. "Hell, yes," he told his partner.

"Huh. You sound cranky. Ms. Kincaid doing yoga again?"

"Nope, cleaning the rain gutters."

"Darn. I won't hurry then. But call me if she starts up with the yoga." AJ's tone revealed the man was no doubt sporting a huge grin. "You know," AJ added, "I can't see Grier staying away from her for much longer. We already know he was infatuated with Nurse Hottie, and seriously, with that bod, who could blame the guy?"

Oh, Caleb couldn't blame Patrick Grier for craving Marley's extremely delectable body, either. Thanks to all the cameras Caleb and AJ had set up around the perimeter of Marley's house providing visuals of the kitchen, living room and bedroom, Caleb had firsthand experience with Kincaid's assets. And he was doing a little bit of craving himself.

Fortunately, all it took was one swift glance at the picture taped to the side of his computer monitor, and the need for vengeance replaced his desire.

As Caleb hung up the phone, he stared at Patrick Grier's grainy features. What pissed him off the most was how normal Grier looked. Brown hair, brown eyes, handsome in a preppy sort of way. That was drug-dealing murderers for you—they rarely ever looked like the scum they were.

If it were any other scumbag dealer, Caleb might have handed the case over to a junior agent and focused on the bigger fish swimming around in the drug pond. But this particular scumbag had murdered Caleb's best friend, and he wasn't going to rest until Patrick Grier was behind bars.

He looked back at the monitor and grinned when he noticed Marley leaning to the side, one slender arm stretched out as she attempted to tackle a clump of leaves that refused to dislodge. The grin faded, however, when something caught his eye. One of the rungs on the ladder looked...wrong. He leaned closer, squinting at the screen.

"Damn it," he muttered under his breath.

Sure enough, the rung he'd noticed was sagging on one side. He couldn't see much more than that, but he suspected it was cracked. The thing would probably break the second she stepped on it.

Fortunately Marley's feet were on the rung below the broken one, but the way she was reaching her arms out, it wouldn't be long before she needed some more height to connect with her target.

Crap. What should he do in this situation? Sit around and wait for her to fall?

Caleb gritted his teeth. He couldn't go over there and warn her. Making contact with the person you were watching defeated the entire point of a stakeout. And he wouldn't risk the possibility of losing Grier. In his gut, he knew the other man was bound to show up here. When they'd raided the office Grier had been using for his web design company, they'd found more than a dozen pictures of Marley taped on the walls. Grier was obsessed with her, and Caleb knew he'd come for her.

He felt it deep in his gut, a certainty his supervisor, unfortunately, didn't quite agree with. But at least Agent Stevens had green-lighted this stakeout. How long he'd let it go on, Caleb wasn't sure, but for now, he could sit tight and see if his hunch played out. The local cops were already watching Marley at the hospital, but Caleb knew Grier wouldn't make a move there. Too many witnesses around. Here, though... Marley lived alone, didn't have many visitors and her house sat at the end of a cul-de-sac with a large park right behind it. This was the perfect place for Grier to make an appearance.

On the screen, Marley was looking up at the roof in dismay. An ominous feeling crept along Caleb's spine. He watched as she lifted one foot. His chest tightened with sickly anticipation.

"Don't do it," he mumbled at her, though of course she couldn't hear him. "Look down first."

But she didn't, and it was like seeing the chain of events that led up to a disaster, in slow motion, unable to do a damn thing about it.

She climbed up onto the next rung of the ladder, and he could practically hear the wood splintering beneath her feet. He couldn't see her face, but he could imagine the look of terror filling her pretty features as the rung gave way. She lost her footing, and the ladder swiftly toppled onto the grass down below.

Caleb shot to his feet, adrenaline pumping through his veins. A faint flicker of admiration lit his chest as he saw her arms whip up like an acrobat's, grabbing at the white-painted eave.

Relief flooded through him. She hadn't fallen. Instead, she dangled ten feet off the ground like a really crappy cat burglar attempting to scale a building. Caleb couldn't help but grin at the thought, but his mouth hardened when Marley twisted her neck, glancing down at the grass as if contemplating whether she could land the jump.

Sure you can, sweetheart, except you'll probably break your ankle. Or your neck.

Letting out a sigh, Caleb took one last look at the screen, then tore out of the room.

He ran out the front door of the house the agency had rented from a pair of retired teachers who were traveling for the summer. The afternoon sun nearly blinded him, making him realize he hadn't been outside in a week. It felt weird after being cooped up indoors for so long.

He crossed the perfectly kept lawn toward the side of the house. Only a couple of yards separated the two homes, and when he approached, Marley still hung from the eaves, cursing to herself under her breath.

He cleared his throat. "Need some help?"

She yelped in surprise and nearly lost her grip. Her legs swung wildly, making his heartbeat quicken. "Don't let go," he ordered.

"Who are you?" Her voice sounded tinny as it floated down from above.

"Your next-door neighbor," he replied. "And possibly the guy who saves your life."

She peered down at him, her light-brown eyes narrowed with suspicion. "I know my next-door neighbors, mister, and you aren't them."

"The Strathorns are in Europe. I'm renting their house for the summer," he called back, annoyance tightening his lips. "Now, do you think we can discuss this *after* we get you down from there?"

There was a long pause. Then she was scrutinizing the ground again. "I think I can make the jump," she said. "I once saw a documentary on stunt doubles."

He suppressed a laugh. "That's terrific. But no, you cannot make the jump." He swallowed. "I'll catch you."

She let out a squeaky protest. "What? No way. What if you miss? Or what if I crush you—"

"With the hundred pounds you're packing?" he interrupted in amusement. "You won't crush me, and I won't miss."

Caleb stepped closer, assessing the height and angle from which she was hanging. If he raised his arms, he could almost touch her sneakers. "I'll catch you," he said with confidence. "I need you to take a deep breath, and let go. Okay?"

"No, thanks."

He closed his eyes briefly, fighting back irritation. "What do you mean, no thanks?" He scowled up at her. "Are you always so difficult?"

"No, I'm scared," she retorted. "I'm only twenty-seven. I don't want to die today."

This time he couldn't stop a laugh from rumbling out of his throat. "You won't die. Trust me. Deep breath, then let go. On the count of three, okay?"

She hesitated for what seemed like an eternity. "Okay."

He rubbed his hands together, widening his stance. "One," he called. "Two—"

"Wait—on three, or one, two, three, let go?"

Caleb sighed. "On three."

"Fine."

He started again. "One...two...*three*."

A second later, her body came flying down and he suddenly found himself with an armful of warm, soft woman. One hand had instinctively reached out to cup her bottom, and his palm now cradled a firm, perfectly round backside, as Marley Kincaid's arms wound tightly around his neck.

She was breathing heavily, her body trembling a little. "You all right?" he asked. His voice sounded rough even to his own ears.

She nodded, tilting her head to look up at him. Her brown eyes widened slightly, her lips parting in surprise as she examined his face. She checked him out for so long he felt a pang of discomfort. "You should really let someone else clean those gutters for you," he grumbled.

Marley just stared at him, and then, to his extreme confusion, she started to laugh.

2

"SERIOUSLY," HER SEXY SAVIOR said in a deep voice. "If you don't tell me you're okay in the next two seconds, I'm calling an ambulance."

"I'm okay," she sputtered.

God, this was priceless. Her laughter came out in soft waves, while adrenaline still pumped through her blood. She suddenly wondered if Gwen had somehow planned this, though that seemed totally unlikely. But come on, what were the chances? Her friend had been babbling about tall, dark, handsome strangers sweeping Marley off her feet, and all of a sudden, a tall, dark, handsome stranger shows up and sweeps her off her feet. Literally.

"Can I let you go now?" he asked, a tad brusquely.

Her laughter finally trailed off. She nodded, and he set her down. Her legs were still quite shaky after her brush with possible death, but her brain seemed to have forgotten about her roof gymnastics—it was too busy analyzing the beautiful man standing in front of her.

He had that chiseled kind of face you expected to see on a movie screen, lines and angles put together to create a rugged landscape, vivid eyes the color of the Pacific Ocean. A pair of faded jeans clung to his long legs and taut behind, while a navy-blue T-shirt emphasized a broad chest and delicious set of rippled abs.

No doubt about it, this was one ridiculously gorgeous man.

Her heart did a few somersaults. "Thanks for catching me," she said.

"No problem." He took a step backward, looking like he couldn't wait to get out of here. "Be more careful next time, all right?" Another step. "I'll see you around."

"Wait, who did you say you were again?"

"I'm Caleb Ford." His blue eyes flickering with weariness, he extended his hand. "I'm renting the house next door to yours." As if to confirm it, he gestured to the redbrick side wall of the Strathorn house.

Since he was sticking his hand out at her, she had no choice but to shake it. The moment they touched, warmth suffused her palm, followed by a spark of awareness. Gosh, this guy was attractive. The messy black hair, the serious blue eyes, the drool-worthy bod. And his hand felt good on hers. Too good.

She quickly snatched it away, leery of the awareness sliding around in her body. Fine, so this guy was incredibly handsome, but he was also a total stranger. And the Strathorns hadn't told her they were renting their place out for the summer. She knew they were in Europe—they'd asked her to pick up their mail. So why hadn't they mentioned someone named Caleb Ford would be staying in their house?

"How do you know the Strathorns?"

Her voice held a note of suspicion, which she didn't attempt to hide. Since her experience with Patrick, she was far more careful about handing out her trust to strangers.

"Through a mutual friend. I heard they were going to Europe for a few months, so my friend arranged for me to rent this place while they're gone."

"Oh, that's convenient." She casually pushed a strand of blond hair off her forehead. Her ponytail had pretty much come apart after her near fall, and unruly blond waves kept getting in her eyes. "Isn't Stan and Debbie's house terrific? They have a lot of antiques in there."

Caleb arched one dark brow. "*Stu* and Debbie, you mean."

"Right, Stu, I don't know why I said Stan." She felt a little flustered, especially when a knowing glint filled his eyes. He knew exactly what she'd tried to do, but hey, at least he'd passed the test. So why was he still all fidgety?

"When did you say you moved in?" she asked, watching him carefully.

"I didn't. But it's been a week."

A week? And she hadn't seen him even once? She tried to rein in her misgivings. Okay, so maybe he didn't leave the house a lot. He could be one of those hermit types who liked being alone indoors.

"And you're here for the summer?" she said, trying to sound casual.

"Yep."

"On vacation?" she pressed.

"Work-related, actually."

For Pete's sake, getting answers from this man was like pulling teeth. She paused for a second, trying to concoct a way to draw some more details out of him, when a flash of red caught her eye. She glanced down, surprised to see an angry-looking scrape on her upper arm. She must have cut herself when she'd grabbed for the ledge, or maybe on her way down into Caleb's arms.

"Shoot, I should get this cleaned up," she said.

"Do you need any help?"

His voice was so full of reluctance she almost felt insulted. Jeez, was the thought of spending even a few more minutes with her that unappealing?

She frowned. "I'm a nurse, I can take care of it. But thanks."

Caleb slung his hands in the pockets of his jeans, shifting awkwardly. "You better go in and get that taken care of. Are you sure you didn't hurt yourself anywhere else?"

She examined her arms and legs, then flexed her back, wincing when a jolt of pain sliced up her left shoulder. "I think I pulled a muscle," she answered, "but it's nothing some yoga can't fix this evening."

Caleb coughed abruptly.

"Are *you* okay?" she asked, wrinkling her brow.

"Yeah, I'm, uh, fine." He began to inch away again. Lord, the way this guy acted, it was as if she was carrying the Ebola virus or something. "I really do have to go. Take care of yourself, uh...?"

"Marley," she supplied.

"Marley," he echoed. He lifted his hand, giving a stilted wave and a brisk nod, and then hurried off with long, smooth strides.

She watched as he walked away, shaking her head to herself. He disappeared around the side of the house and a few moments later, she heard the Strathorns' front door shut.

Okay. Well, that was kind of weird. He was probably

telling the truth, and really was renting the house next door, but maybe she ought to call the number Debbie had left for her just to make sure Caleb Ford was who he said he was. He'd been acting a little odd for her liking.

Yeah, she definitely should call, she decided as she bent down to take care of the ladder. She pushed it to the wall, leaning it length-wise against the house, then glanced down at her arm, which was beginning to ooze blood.

With a sigh, she headed into the house, making a mental note to contact Debbie Strathorn as soon as possible. Caleb Ford might be drop-dead gorgeous, but he was still a stranger.

And these days, Marley's guard went on high alert when it came to sexy men who made her heart skip a beat.

A girl couldn't be too cautious, after all.

"So...WHAT WAS *THAT* ABOUT?"

Caleb nearly tripped over his own feet at the sound of AJ's voice. He'd expected to find the master bedroom empty, but AJ was casually sitting at the desk, sipping from a tall Starbucks cup.

With his military-style buzz cut, tattooed arms and black leather jacket, Adam James Callaghan looked like the type of guy Caleb would be slapping handcuffs on and dragging to jail.

But AJ was a damn good agent, a bit of a legend around the Drug Enforcement Agency. He'd spent three years undercover with a Colombian drug cartel, which was how he'd gotten all the tattoos. Had to prove himself, show he was one of them, AJ had told Caleb. He'd also managed to gather enough evidence to take down the entire organization. But now he was stateside, assigned as Caleb's new partner.

Caleb walked over to the desk and peered at the monitors, instantly spotting Marley in the kitchen. She was pulling a first-aid kit out of the cupboard under the sink.

"What was what about?" he asked, absently reaching for one of the steaming cups sitting in the cardboard tray on the desk.

AJ shot him a look loaded with disbelief. "You know exactly what I'm talking about. I come back from a coffee run to find—"

"You came in from the back, right?" Caleb cut in.

"Yes, I came in from the back. Same way I've been coming in for the past week. And yes, I parked the car two streets over. And no, nobody saw me when I cut through the park on my way here." AJ frowned. "Now quit interrogating me and tell me what the hell you were thinking, making contact with Kincaid."

Caleb walked over to the king-size bed and sank down onto the edge. "She fell off a ladder."

AJ swiveled his chair around to face him. "She fell off a ladder," he repeated.

"Yes, but she managed to hang on to the roof. She would have fallen off that, too, if I hadn't gone out to help her." The defensive note in his voice made him want to cringe, but he knew AJ's thoughts on the subject of Marley Kincaid. And none of them were too positive.

AJ put down his coffee cup in obvious annoyance. "Just in case you've forgotten, we're on a stakeout, man. The whole point of a stakeout is remaining out of sight, inconspicuous."

"I know that," Caleb ground out. "But what did you want me to do, watch her tumble to her death?"

"What I want you to do is focus on the bastard that killed one of our own." AJ frowned. "I've seen the way you look at her, Caleb, and I don't particularly like it, all right? She might very well be helping Grier and you know it."

"Yes, and she might not be helping him," Caleb countered, meeting his partner's hard gaze with one of his own.

"Then explain the hundred grand that was wired into her bank account after the DEA got the tip that Grier was heading to San Diego."

"It was a joint account, you know that. Grier could've made the deposit as easily as Kincaid."

"And she has no knowledge of what's going on in her own bank accounts? If a hundred thousand dollars mysteriously wound up in my account, I'd be talking to the bank, or calling the cops. Unless I know my slime-bag ex put it in there, and I'm planning on helping him get out of the country."

Caleb's jaw tightened at the thought of Grier taking off and disappearing. Oh, no, not happening. Caleb would catch the son of a bitch long before that happened. The DEA finally had hard evidence on the guy, after years of being unable to bring charges against the supposed web designer. Three months ago, an informant inside the Ruiz cartel—the Brazilian outfit they'd been trying to bust for years—had provided information about a shipment Grier was scheduled to distribute for the Ruizes.

Only, the raid they'd organized hadn't gone as planned, and Grier had yet again escaped arrest.

"If she's helping Grier, we'll find out," Caleb replied.

"All I'm saying is that we shouldn't jump to conclusions. Maybe she's involved, maybe she's not. But don't paint her with Grier's brush until we have some proof."

Even as he said the words, he knew AJ wouldn't heed them. His partner believed in Marley's guilt. Caleb, on the other hand...he was ninety percent sure Marley wasn't involved in any of this. He didn't quite believe Marley was in cahoots with Grier now, or that she'd been aware of his actions then. Grier was smooth, and according to his file, he'd fooled women before. Killed them, too, or at least he'd been suspected of it.

Still, ninety percent meant there was still that ten percent of doubt floating around in his head. He didn't want to believe Marley was somehow funneling money into her ex's hands, but it wasn't something he could rule out, either. At least their presence next door ensured they'd see Grier if he showed up.

"And if she's not involved," Caleb added, "she could be in danger. You know what happened to Grier's previous girlfriend."

"Yeah, she found out he was a criminal and tried to help the cops."

"Her dead body wound up in a Dumpster in Nevada, for Chrissake."

AJ sighed. "And I'm sorry that happened to her, but at least she was trying to take down Grier. Kincaid, on the other hand... I don't know, man, the hundred grand in that bank account makes me mighty reluctant to trust her."

"Well, you don't have to trust her. You just need to watch her." Unwittingly, Caleb snuck another peek at the monitor, where Marley had finished bandaging her cut. She was now in the second-floor bedroom, fixing her ponytail.

He wished he could find out exactly what was going on in her head. He needed to know more than what these brief glimpses provided. First and foremost, had she truly been oblivious to her fiancé's criminal activities?

Yet there were other questions he'd also love to get the answers to. Like what had she seen in Grier in the first place? Why was she doing all these renovations on her house by herself? What did she look like naked?

Caleb stifled a groan. It always seemed to come back to that, didn't it? Marley Kincaid's incredibly appealing body. It was the tease of watching, but not really *seeing*. Catching glimpses of her breasts in silhouette, but never knowing exactly what color her nipples were, never knowing how those firm mounds would feel in his palms or rubbing against his chest, pressed up to his mouth....

Jeez, AJ was right. This attraction really was getting out of hand.

"Grier will show up soon," Caleb declared. "Whether Marley is helping him doesn't matter. My gut tells me he's going to come for her."

AJ didn't look convinced. "You know I usually have the utmost respect for an agent's gut, but how are you so sure? I've read his file, Caleb, and he doesn't form attachments. He uses people, then walks away."

"She's different." Caleb's voice grew quiet. "He never moved in with anyone before, never proposed marriage, never opened a damned joint savings account. I'm telling you, AJ, he'll come for her."

"He'd better," AJ said with a trace of bitterness. "That bastard needs to pay for what he did to Russ."

The sound of Russ's name brought a deep ache to Caleb's chest. He hadn't had many friends growing up—being carted from foster home to foster home put a cramp in a guy's social life—but Russell Delacroix had been the exception. Caleb had met Russ at a group home when he was sixteen, and the two of them developed a friendship that had thrived for years. Russ had been the one who convinced him to join the DEA, and they'd been partners for eight years.

As long as he lived, Caleb knew he'd never forget the sight of Russ's body crumpling to the cold ground of that warehouse three months ago. Even now, the memory of Russ's blood staining the dirty floor sent a wave of rage through Caleb's gut.

Russ had been family, a brother. And losing him to a drug dealer had been a crushing blow.

Caleb tried to swallow the ball of fury lodged in his throat. "He'll pay," he said hoarsely. "He *will* show up here, I know it, and when he does, we'll be waiting."

AJ leaned back in the chair, giving a satisfied nod. "Nice to hear you have your priorities straight."

Caleb bristled. "What's that supposed to mean?"

"It means that you've been lusting after your cute nurse for a week now, and I'm glad you're still able to remember why we're here." AJ's voice took on an admiring note. Glancing at the screen, he let out a soft whistle. "Though I've gotta admit, she's fun to watch."

Caleb followed AJ's gaze, then stifled a groan. Marley had just come out of the walk-in closet in her bedroom, wearing black Spandex pants that hugged her shapely legs, while a tight yellow tank top stretched across her full, perky breasts.

Caleb's fingers curled into fists. A jolt of desire shot straight to his cock and turned it to granite. He knew Marley's routine to a T now, and when she put on the Spandex…that meant only one thing was about to happen.

Sexy yoga time.

He tore his eyes off the screen. "Have you made any progress figuring out where the money came from?"

AJ shook his head. "Still can't trace it."

Releasing a heavy breath, Caleb got to his feet and approached the desk. "Then we keep waiting."

"So, what, we sit around for another week, waiting for something to happen? How long is Stevens going to let this stakeout go on?"

"I don't know. But as long as we're here, all we *can* do is wait."

"For what?" AJ sounded frustrated. "There's been no activity in the account since the wire transfer, no appearances by Grier, no phone calls, nada. What do you suggest we do?"

"We keep watching," Caleb said, shrugging.

You mean torturing yourself.

He allowed himself another peek at the screen, swallowing when he noticed the sensual workout had begun. She always started out with sexy stretches that showcased her legs and emphasized her sleek calf muscles, followed by a series of little pelvic tilts that never failed to hold his undivided attention. *Oh, and look at that, now she had her hands and feet on the mat, ass thrust up into the air.*

Caleb smothered a groan. How much more of this could he take? He was only a man, after all. A thirty-one-year-old single man who'd always had a healthy appetite when it came to sex.

And the woman on the screen, with her lithe body and floor gymnastics, just screamed sex. The proximity of their houses, separated by mere yards, only made the situation worse. It was only ten steps from his porch to hers. Ten steps, and he could be at her door…in her bed…

"Maybe making contact wasn't such a bad idea," AJ said suddenly.

Caleb's head jerked up. "What are you talking about? You just chewed me out for that."

"Yeah, but I'm looking at it from another angle. You already laid some of the groundwork today," AJ said, a thoughtful look entering his harsh features. "You saved her life, chatted her up. Sure, she thinks you're a total weirdo, but—"

"What do you mean, she thinks I'm a weirdo?"

His partner shrugged. "You were like a panicked little rabbit out there. Seriously, you kept inching away, like you were going to bolt any second. I saw the look on her face, man. She's suspicious of you. And she thinks you're weird." AJ offered a big grin. "Fortunately, you're going to fix that by going over there tomorrow."

Caleb faltered. He didn't reply for a moment, running the idea through his mind. "No," he finally said.

"Why not? All you've gotta do is befriend her, get her to open up and figure out what she knows about Grier."

AJ made it sound like the easiest task on the planet, which, for AJ, it probably was. Despite his scary biker looks, AJ was never hurting for female company. Not Caleb, though. His problem wasn't finding female company; it was making sure nobody ever got too close. He liked his women the way he liked his cars—fast, bold and temporary. No strings, no hassles and definitely no relationships. He'd learned the hard way the price you paid when you formed attachments to people.

And he didn't want to get close to Marley Kincaid. His attraction to her had already proven too big a hassle—why make it worse?

"I won't sleep with her to find out what she knows about Grier," he grumbled.

"Who said anything about sleeping with her? Uh, one-track mind?" AJ snorted. "All I said was become friends with her. She cut her arm, right? Go over there tomorrow to make sure she's okay."

Caleb studied the monitor with a frown. The bedroom was now empty, but light spilled from underneath the closed bathroom door. Another part of the routine, a long shower after sexy yoga.

Indecision rippled inside him. Should he do this? It had been kind of amusing, talking to her outside. She had a great sense of humor, and she also happened to be the most beautiful woman Caleb had ever seen. Plus he was wildly attracted to her. An attraction that could equal trouble.

But AJ had a point. Caleb's supervisor, Ken Stevens, was a good man, but he wasn't known for his patience. If this stakeout didn't produce any results, if Grier didn't show up soon, Stevens would pull them out. Making contact with Marley and finding out if she knew anything might help move the case along. Hell, it might be the only way to keep the case alive.

"I guess I can do that," he said slowly. "Just to see if she knows something."

Right, because her fresh-faced beauty and killer body have nothing to do with it.

"You're a professional," AJ said, as if he knew where Caleb's thoughts had drifted. "Keep it casual, dig around and hopefully she leads us to Grier."

"And if she doesn't?"

AJ let out a frustrated sigh that revealed precisely how he felt about his next words. "Then we go back to waiting."

EMERGING FROM THE SHADOWS, Patrick Grier deftly hopped the fence leading into the backyard of the house across the street from Marley's. Darkness bathed the yard, which only helped his cause as he crept toward the back door. He'd purposely waited for the sun to set, killing time on a pier a few miles from here. He couldn't risk anyone seeing him in this neighborhood. A contact of his had warned him the cops were still watching Marley. Otherwise he would've broken into her house months ago. But he had to play it safe. Getting caught wouldn't help him or Marley one damn bit.

The door swung open easily when he turned the knob, and he stepped into the dark house. The temptation to run across the street to see Marley was so strong his legs started to itch. He swiftly fought the urge. He didn't have a death wish, after all.

Breaking into this house had been risky enough, but fortunately he knew the old bat who lived here. He'd spoken to Lydia White several times when he'd lived across the street, and during their talks he'd learned she lived alone and had zero family. No friends, either, though that wasn't a surprise considering her foul personality.

But even bitches had to eat.

Tucking the deli bag under his arm, Patrick headed upstairs without turning on any lights. The spare bedroom at the end of the hall had a perfect view of Marley's place, and when he peeked out the window, he noticed her bedroom light was on. Was she lying in bed, thinking of him?

Turning away from the window, he strode to the narrow closet and flung the door open. A pair of wide brown eyes greeted him, along with the muffled screams of Lydia White as she wiggled around on the closet floor like a scared puppy.

Patrick scrunched up his nose when the faint odor of urine drifted into his nostrils. "You couldn't hold it for a day?" he spat out.

The old lady whimpered, terror filling her wrinkled face.

Gritting his teeth, Patrick bent down and hauled her up so that she was sitting. He yanked off the duct tape stuck to her mouth. "Open your mouth, I brought you some grub. And remember what I said about screaming." As a reminder, he half turned to show her the black 9mm sticking out of his waistband.

Another whimper.

Ripping the wax paper covering the ham sandwich he'd picked up, he lifted one half to the lady's mouth and practically forced it down her wrinkled old throat. She objected at first, but then began to chew, unable to resist the first form of nourishment she'd had since he'd left the house early this morning.

He stifled a curse as he fed the old bat, wishing he could just kill her and be done with it. But he wasn't a cold-blooded murderer. No, he only killed when his own survival was threatened. Besides, he needed old Lydia around to answer the phone when some rare person called—while Patrick held a gun to her head, of course.

So far, Lydia had followed instructions like a pro. And using her house as his base of operations was ideal. For the moment.

"Here," he barked, uncapping a bottle of water and bringing it to Lydia's mouth.

The elderly woman drank fervently, but the glimmer of fear never once left her eyes.

"Don't look at me like that," he snapped. "I told you, I won't be here long. I'm just making some arrangements and then I'll be gone."

And so would Marley. No way was he leaving her behind. She was the love of his life, after all. So unbelievably different from the fast and loose women in his past. He'd known it the second she'd walked into his hospital room in her green scrubs, with that gentle smile on her face.

His smile dissolved into a frown as he thought about all the shit that had gone down three months ago. He still experienced an onslaught of rage every time he remembered what had happened in the warehouse. Damn cops. The shipment they'd intercepted had cost him millions of dollars. Not to mention that they'd officially made it impossible for him ever to live in the States again.

Tomorrow morning, he planned on driving to Tijuana to meet with a guy who was arranging the necessary papers, and he was still working on a way to contact Marley. Once he did, he could get hold of the money he'd hidden in her house. He'd stashed two hundred grand under her bathroom floor three days after he moved in; it was part of his routine—always have an exit strategy in case you need one.

And then there was the hundred grand in his and Marley's joint account. Earlier this week a European contact who owed him money had transferred the dough in there, since the feds had frozen all of Patrick's personal accounts and he didn't have the resources yet to open anything new. He wasn't sure why they'd left the joint account open—his instincts told him it was a trap—but if he could, he planned on transferring the amount to a bank in the Caymans when he secured the necessary ID papers.

Once he got the cash from Marley's house, though, he was outta here.

And Marley was going with him.

Sure she is, came the cynical voice in his head. *Women always love men who betray them.*

"She *does* love me," Patrick insisted, wishing he could punch that bothersome voice. "And she'll forgive me for lying to her. Marley doesn't stay angry at people, it's not her way."

He noticed the old lady staring up at him with eyes as big as saucers. Had he spoken out loud?

"She does, you know," he said to Lydia. "Love me, I mean."

The certainty surrounding his heart was as strong as steel, causing the worry in his gut to dissolve. Of course Marley would forgive him. She was still his. All he had to do was find a way to get to her. And once he had the cash, he was going to whisk Marley away to a place where nobody could ever tear them apart again.

3

"OKAY, SO HERE'S WHAT you're going to do," Gwen said, tightening the drawstring on her bright pink scrubs.

Marley flopped onto the narrow bench in the nurse's locker room and bent down to untie her shoelaces. "What are you talking about?"

"Your neighbor."

"You're still hung up on this?" Marley frowned. "I told you, he's kind of strange."

"But you said he was cute." Gwen grinned. "And he caught you when you did a swan dive off the roof."

"Fine, he gets two points for that. And then minus three points for being aloof. I swear, he couldn't wait to get away from me."

"But you spoke to Debbie, right?"

Marley nodded. "Before I left for work. She said she and Stu did rent the house, to a writer from New York, and, yes, his name is Caleb Ford."

"Well, there you go, he was telling the truth."

"Yeah, but… Something about him was really off."

"So he's shy. Which is why you need to make a move," Gwen answered as she tied her curly hair in a loose twist at the top of her head. "Tonight you're going to walk next door and ask for a cup of sugar."

Marley laughed. "No way. That's so lame."

"Wait, I'm not done. So you ask for the sugar, and then you bat your eyelashes and say, 'Actually, maybe I can give *you* some sugar instead.' One thing will lead to another and presto! You get laid and forget all about Patrick."

Marley shot her friend a firm look. "I'm not going to seduce my neighbor."

"Then at least promise to keep an open mind," Gwen pleaded. "There's no harm in saying hi to the guy next time you see him. Just don't be afraid of some flirting, or heck, even a casual conversation. Oh, and could you *please* come out with me and Nick on Tuesday? We're going to the salsa bar. It'll be a good time."

"I'll let you know." Marley took a step toward the locker room door. "I gotta go. My feet are killing me and I'm craving a long, hot bubble bath."

Gwen sighed. "I hate the night shift," she complained as she followed Marley out the door. "You're so lucky you're going home."

"Yeah, to sleep," she replied with a sigh. "I'm coming back for the graveyard shift, while you get to spend the night with your boyfriend."

"Good point."

They said goodbye in the hallway, and Marley headed for the elevator, her flip-flops snapping against the white linoleum floor.

When she exited the hospital, the early-evening air was warm, and she breathed it in, enjoying the fresh scent of salt and palm trees. She loved San Diego—the heat, the laid-back atmosphere, the ocean. She hadn't been to the beach in ages, she realized as she crossed

the parking lot to her car. The renovations in her house
were tedious and left little time for trips to the beach.

But maybe Gwen was right. Maybe it was time to
quit using her house as an excuse not to go out and
have fun. God knew she needed some fun after the
past year.

Before she could start the car, her cell phone burst
out in the Pussycat Dolls ringtone Gwen had down-
loaded as a joke. Her brother's number flashed on the
screen, causing Marley to stifle a groan. Sam still
hadn't come back to finish the closet he'd half gutted,
and she had a feeling she was in for another excuse.

Sighing, she lifted the phone to her ear. "Hey,
Sammy. What's up?"

"I wanted to touch base with you about the closet."

"Finally. So when are you coming to finish it?"

"That's what I wanted to talk about. It'll probably
have to be at the end of the week."

"Why not earlier?"

"No time. We've got a massive renovation to finish
this week, kiddo."

Marley rolled her eyes. "Don't call me kiddo. I'm
three years older than you, Sammy."

"On paper, maybe. But in maturity, I win."

"In your dreams."

"See how immature you are? Only ten-year-olds say
'in your dreams.'" He suddenly sounded contrite. "I'll
try to make it earlier, since you're being so difficult."

"What's difficult is having to jump over a huge hole
in the floor every time I walk down my hall," she countered.

"I'll fix it soon, I promise. Anyway, I've gotta go.
We'll talk this week, 'kay?"

"Hot date?" she teased.

"Yep."

Marley grinned to herself. "Should I bother asking for her name or will she be but a mere speed bump in the road that is your love life?"

"Very poetic. And the answer is we'll see," Sam said mysteriously. "I'll talk to you later, kiddo."

They hung up, and Marley was still smiling as she started the car and left the hospital staff lot. Sam always managed to brighten her day. They hadn't been very close growing up. He'd been the epitome of a pesky little brother, what with his unfunny pranks and that God-awful, year-long "why?" phase. Oh, and she most definitely hadn't appreciated the time he'd squeezed purple hair dye into her shampoo bottle. *Permanent* hair dye. But after their mother died, they'd banded together to console their dad, and a bond had formed. Now, Marley couldn't imagine not having Sammy in her life.

Turning onto the main street, she headed in the direction of home. As she pulled into her driveway, she noticed a shiny black Range Rover parked next door and her heart gave an involuntary jump. She thought of Caleb Ford's piercing blue eyes and lean, muscular body, then pushed the memory of her neighbor from her mind. She parked and climbed the rickety porch steps, her feet aching the entire time. Forget yoga tonight—she was heading straight to the bathtub and staying in there for hours.

Kicking off her flip-flops, she closed the door, hopped over the stack of two-by-fours on the floor and made a beeline for the narrow staircase. The moment she reached the top step, the doorbell chimed, startling the hell out of her.

Sighing, she headed back downstairs, determined

to get rid of whoever had rung the bell. No one she knew would show up unannounced, so it was probably someone selling newspaper subscriptions or something equally annoying, and she wasn't in the mood to deal with that right now. She paused in front of the door and peered into the peephole.

A shaky breath flew out of her mouth when she found Caleb Ford's blue eyes peering back at her.

Shoot. She was so not prepared for a visit from the hottie next door. She had convertible hair, wasn't wearing a spot of makeup and she hadn't even bothered putting on a bra when she'd changed out of her nursing scrubs.

But she couldn't *not* answer the door. He knew she was home. He'd probably seen her pull up just now.

The doorbell rang a second time.

Maybe she shouldn't answer it all. She didn't know this guy—just because he was renting the house next door, that didn't make them buddies. She didn't owe him anything.

Actually, you do. He helped you escape death.

A sharp knock rapped against the door, making her jump. Wow, this guy was overeager, wasn't he?

Taking a deep breath, she finally reached for the knob and opened the door. And then there he was, standing on her porch and looking even sexier than she remembered.

He hooked his thumbs through the belt loops of his faded blue jeans. The stance just screamed *cool,* emphasized by the way the sun was setting directly behind him. Dark oranges and reds lit up the sky, and in turn cast a ruddy glow over him. He looked like a cowboy in the Wild West, standing in the sunset.

Vivid imagination, Marley.

"Did I catch you at a bad time?" Caleb asked in a deep sexy voice that made her shiver despite the balmy breeze drifting into the hall.

She shook the cobwebs from her mind and tried to remember what she'd been doing before being assaulted by his sex appeal. "I was about to take a bath," she admitted.

Something flickered in his eyes. Heat?

"Oh." He cleared his throat. "Sorry I interrupted you. I came by to see about your arm."

"My arm?" Then she remembered, and glanced down at the bandage covering the cut. "It's fine, just a scrape."

"Oh," he said again, shifting awkwardly. "I guess I'll go then. I just wanted to see how you were doing."

Promise to keep an open mind. Be open to some flirting, or heck, even a casual conversation.

Gwen's words buzzed in her head. She hesitated. Okay, maybe she could manage some light-hearted small talk, a flirty remark or two. It wouldn't kill her. He was obviously trying to be nice, coming over to check on her.

Besides, did she really want to send away the first man who'd made her feel anything close to desire in months?

"The bath can wait a little while longer," she found herself saying. "Do you want to come in for a quick cup of coffee?"

He nodded. "Sure, if it's no trouble."

"None at all." She opened the door wider. As he stepped into her narrow front hall, she felt overpowered by the sheer maleness of him. He was at least six-two, his big firm body dominating the small space. Before she could stop herself, she imagined that big firm body dominating *her,* and her breasts immediately ached, her nipples poking out against the front of her tank top. She wasn't surprised when Caleb's eyes dropped to her chest, lingering only for a second.

And with that one brief look, a rush of heat filled her body. She was rooted in place, watching his face as he watched her, and for a moment she experienced a sense of familiarity. As if they knew each other. There was something unbelievably intimate about his gaze.

She cleared her throat. "Uh, the kitchen's this way."

Caleb followed her down the hall, keeping a respectful distance behind her. As they entered her kitchen, she experienced a twinge of embarrassment at the chaos in the large airy space. Last weekend she'd scraped off most of the awful flower-patterned wallpaper the previous owners had described as *charming* in the real estate listing, and the walls were now bare. Paint cans sat near the splintered oak counter, which she needed to replace, and since she planned on painting the pantry, too, all the food from there rested in boxes against the wall. The room was a disaster.

"Sorry for the mess," she apologized. "I'm doing some renovating."

He raised a brow. "On your own?"

"Yep," she replied, gesturing for him to sit at the table tucked in the corner of the room. "I'm about to start the kitchen, which leaves me with, oh, every other room in the house."

Caleb's mouth lifted in a crooked smile. Marley's breath caught in her throat. Wow. This man definitely needed to do that more often.

He sank into one of the tall-backed chairs and crossed his ankles. "You're a do-it-yourself type then."

"Of course. It's not fun hiring someone to do the job

for you." She shrugged. "Way more satisfying knowing that I did the work."

She flicked on the coffeemaker and opened the cupboard above the sink, pulling out two mugs. "So what brought a New Yorker all the way across the country?"

There was a long pause, and then he chuckled. "Checking up on me, huh?"

She turned around and met his knowing look. "What?"

"I never told you I was from New York."

Heat scorched her cheeks. Shoot. Totally busted. How could she slip up like that?

"I called Debbie in Paris," she admitted. "I just wanted to make sure you were on the up and up. They didn't mention a renter before they left."

"It was a last-minute thing," he said, not offering further explanation.

The coffee machine clicked, and she poured the hot liquid into the mugs, glancing over at him. "Let me guess, you take yours black."

His lips twitched. "How'd you know?"

"Just a feeling." She dumped two spoonfuls of sugar into her cup, then walked over to the table and handed him his. Rather than sitting, she leaned against the counter again, blowing on her coffee to cool it.

"You're just going to hover over me like that?" Caleb asked.

"I hate sitting down," she confessed. "Probably because of my job. I'm on my feet all day, and I've gotten used to it. I go a little stir crazy when I'm in a chair."

"So…" He held his cup in one hand, looking a bit uncomfortable. "Do you usually make sure everyone you meet is on the up and up?"

The blush returned to her cheeks. "Not really. I

just…well, I like the Strathorns and I wanted to make sure…" Her voice trailed, and she made a wry face. "Sorry, I guess I've been having some trust issues lately."

He appeared to mull over her remark, then raised his mug to his lips. She watched his throat work as he swallowed, her stomach doing a funny little flip. Caleb Ford oozed masculinity, even when he drank. She couldn't help wondering if he'd be like that in bed, controlled, powerful.

As if he'd read her mind, he locked his eyes with hers. Little sparks danced along Marley's skin. There were sparks in the air, too. Hard to ignore them, zinging back and forth between her and Caleb, heating her skin. Breaking the eye contact, she distracted herself by taking another sip of coffee.

"Yeah, I know all about those. Trust issues," he clarified with a shrug. "To be honest, trust isn't something I'm good at."

She was suddenly curious. "Giving it, or getting it?"

"A little of both, probably."

Before she could press for details, he glanced around the room, taking in the paint supplies scattered on the tiled floor. "So you're starting with the painting first?" When she nodded, he said, "What else are you planning to do?"

Considering the grief Gwen had given her about these renovations yesterday, it was nice talking to someone who actually seemed interested. Before she could stop herself, she launched into a recitation of everything she planned to fix up. She was vaguely aware that she'd gone into babbling mode, but hey, at least it helped her ignore the rampant flames of sexual attraction threatening to burn down her kitchen.

CALEB WAS HAVING a very tough time keeping his eyes off Marley. Leaning against the counter in her faded jeans and curve-hugging tank top, with her golden hair up in a messy ponytail and her bare feet, she made a seriously alluring picture.

Her mere proximity made his body burn. Despite the odor of paint fumes lingering in the air, he could also make out a more subtle fragrance. Strawberries. The feminine aroma drove him wild. So did her legs, encased in that stretchy denim, and damn but she had cute feet—small and dainty with bright-pink toenails.

He imagined those legs wrapped around him, her heels digging into his buttocks, and fought back a moan.

It had been a mistake coming here. He was pretty good at talking women into going to bed with him, but just talking to them? He sucked at it.

He sipped his coffee, using the pause in the conversation to figure out his next move. Okay, so he'd made contact, but sitting around in Marley's kitchen wouldn't land him any answers. He needed to get her talking about Grier. But though he'd been watching her for more than a week now, to her he was a stranger. And women didn't open up to complete strangers.

He glanced at the sliding door on the other side of the kitchen, pretending to admire her backyard while he planned what to say. The sight of the oak tree in Marley's fenced-in yard brought a flicker of guilt, as he realized AJ had set up one of their cameras in the tree's enormous branches. As if someone wanted to hammer the point home, the branches rustled, sending a few leaves fluttering down to the grass.

Caleb shifted his eyes back to Marley. He opened his mouth to speak only to be interrupted by the ring of his cell phone. "Excuse me," he said as he fished his cell out of his pocket. He glanced at the caller ID, saw AJ's number and stifled a curse. "Do you mind if I take this?"

"Go ahead."

He flipped open the phone and said, "Hey, Vic, what's up?"

"I thought you were going to make contact later tonight," AJ hissed.

"I was, but I decided to work on the chapters earlier," Caleb said smoothly.

AJ let out an expletive. "I need you to get her out of the kitchen."

"Are you still in New York?" From the corner of his eye, he saw Marley discreetly move to the sink to rinse out her mug.

"I'm in the freaking tree out back. Looking at your ugly face as we speak," came the heated whisper.

It took all of Caleb's willpower not to look through the sliding door again. Evidently the rustling he'd seen in the tree hadn't come from a mischievous squirrel. The image of AJ's huge leather-clad body up in those branches nearly brought a laugh to the surface, but he quickly clamped it down.

"What are you doing in Florida?" he asked with great interest. AJ had left the house next door an hour ago to grab some groceries. Now he was in Marley's backyard?

"I was coming back and saw the camera dangling from one of the branches. Must have gotten dislodged. She always goes upstairs and does the yoga/shower thing after work so I figured I had time to fix the camera before she saw it, but then you just *had* to show up and bring her into the kitchen. And now I'm in the tree. The end."

"Bird sanctuary, huh? Can't say that's my cup of tea."

AJ swore again. "Just get her out of the kitchen so I can hightail it back next door."

"Sure thing, Vic. I'll email you the chapters by the end of the week so you'll have them when you get back from your vacation."

Caleb hung up the phone and rose to his feet, just as Marley rounded the counter again. To his dismay, she headed right for the patio door and peered out.

He came up behind her. "What are you looking at?" he asked as casually as he could muster.

"I heard you say something about birds," she answered with a sideways glance. "It reminded me that I haven't put seed in my bird feeder for a few days."

She extended a dainty hand, pointing at the bright red bird feeder hanging from the largest branch on the elm. "I made it myself," she added. "The sparrows love it."

Panic rose up Caleb's spine, mostly because he could now see one of AJ's black biker boots camouflaged in the leaves. "I should go," he burst out.

She wrinkled her brow. "Oh. Okay."

"That phone call," he said in an attempt to explain his abrupt exclamation. "I'm a writer, and my agent reminded me I need to revise a few chapters. So, uh, yeah, I should go do that."

Moving away from the patio door, Marley nodded. "I'll walk you—" She tripped over one of the paint cans on the floor, letting out an unladylike curse as she stumbled forward.

Snapping to action, Caleb reached out to steady her.

And regretted it the second his palms made contact with her hips. Her tank top had ridden up, and he was touching skin. Bare, warm skin, so soft that he hissed in a breath.

"I…" Marley's voice drifted and her mouth fell open when she caught sight of the obvious desire in his eyes.

He could do nothing to hide the swift response. Her flesh felt like heaven under his hands, and that sweet scent wafting into his nose was far too intoxicating.

He coughed ever so slightly. "You all right?"

She nodded wordlessly, then glanced down at his hands, which were still on her waist. God help him, but he couldn't seem to let her go.

And she wasn't complaining. Rather, she shifted so they were face to face. Her liquid brown eyes searched his. "I'm…a klutz," she murmured without breaking the eye contact.

Caleb swallowed, his mouth in desperate need of moisture, his lips in desperate need of *her*. Before he could stop himself, he moved his hand over her hip in a fleeting caress. An unsteady breath slid out of her throat.

Insanity. This was freaking insanity, and he was helpless to stop it. He'd been watching Marley Kincaid for seven days, watching and yearning and fighting the arousal he knew he shouldn't be feeling.

But he couldn't fight it now. Not when she was this close.

As his pulse drummed in his ears, he finally gave up. Screw it. Kissing her was wrong on so many levels, but at this point he didn't care. He wanted her so badly his bones ached.

So he took her.

4

MARLEY LET OUT a little gasp as he captured her mouth with his, but the second their lips met, she melted in his arms. He thrust his fingers into her hair, angling her head for better access, while he slid his other hand to her waist and drew her body to his.

She made a gentle, keening sound against his mouth, and then lifted her arms to his shoulders, pulling him closer. Her lips parted, her tongue darted out to toy with his and Caleb nearly keeled over from the jolt of desire that shot through him.

She tasted incredible. Like coffee, cinnamon and heaven and he couldn't get enough of her. He deepened the kiss, drowning in her scent. Damn it, he hadn't known it would be so uncontrollable.

A muffled thud sounded from outside. Marley must have heard it, too, because her eyelids fluttered open at the same time as his.

And then she was out of his arms.

His arms felt empty without her warm supple body in them, his mouth going dry when seconds before it had been moist from the tip of Marley's tongue teasing his lips. Even as his body tried to recover from that unbelievable kiss, his brain went back to business, directing his line of vision to the now-empty yard. Relief coursed through him. AJ had managed The Great Escape.

"I'm sorry," he said hoarsely. "I didn't mean to do that."

"I…" She tucked an errant blond strand behind her ear. "It's fine. Just unexpected."

Understatement of the year. What had he been thinking, kissing her? He'd wanted to distract her, and instead, he'd opened Pandora's damn box, because now that he'd tasted Marley, he wanted nothing more than to do it again.

Information. You just need information from her.

Drawing in a breath, Caleb willed his desire away. "I should go," he said.

Something flickered in her eyes. Finally, she just nodded, and they stepped out of the kitchen. He saw her wringing her hands together as she walked. "So you're a writer, huh?"

He almost laughed. It seemed ridiculous making small talk now, after the explosive kiss they'd just shared. "Yeah, I'm, uh, working on my first novel."

"That's cool."

When they reached the front hall, he glanced down at the two-by-fours on the floor, then the gutted closet. "You sure this isn't a safety hazard?" he asked in a dry voice.

She sighed. "My brother keeps promising to finish it, but he never seems to get around to it."

Caleb ran a hand through his hair, pausing near the front door. "I did some construction a few years back."

The admission came out of nowhere, but at least it

wasn't a lie, like his writer cover story. He *had* done a lot of construction before he joined the DEA.

"I could help you with some of the renovations." Gruffly, he added, "If you'd like."

Marley seemed to hesitate. "No, I couldn't let you do that. You're here to work on a novel."

"It's really no trouble." Damn, why was he insisting?

Information.

Right, it had nothing to do with her stunning face and endless supply of curves. He needed to find out what she knew about Grier. If she even knew anything. AJ thought she did, but Caleb wasn't certain, not after he'd spent some time with her. Everything about Marley seemed so genuine, so refreshing. How did she do it, continue to smile and laugh and live her life after what Patrick Grier had done to her? Unless AJ was right, and she was still in contact with Grier, sticking by him, moving money around to help him escape....

Caleb forcibly shoved all the negative thoughts from his brain and focused on Marley. She considered his offer for so long that he grew certain she would say no, thank you. But then she gave a tiny smile and nodded. "Well, my brother's finishing the closet this week, but I could use some help with the painting," she confessed.

"Should I come by tomorrow?" Anticipation rose in his chest. He quickly banished it, trying to remind himself that he wasn't seeing her for pleasure, but business.

"Sure. Let's see…I'm stuck with a graveyard shift tonight. I start at two—" she made a face "—and I'll be home around eleven tomorrow morning. I'll probably pass out for a while when I get back, so how about four?"

"Sounds good."

Laughing, Marley opened the front door for him. "I'm not sure it'll sound as good when I put you to work painting my kitchen."

He gave her a faint smile. "I look forward to it."

Stepping out onto the porch, he thanked her for the coffee. After the door closed behind him, he released a ragged breath. Lord, that kiss. It was a miracle he'd been able to finish the rest of the conversation.

He could still taste her on his lips, and his current state of discomfort made walking next door difficult. He'd never been harder in his life, and if Marley were any other woman, it wouldn't have stopped with one kiss. He felt it in the way she kissed him back and saw it in the disappointment clouding her eyes when they broke apart. If they were different people, he could've buried himself inside her and eased the ache in his groin. But he couldn't. He couldn't sleep with her.

Getting close to her in order to learn the truth was a necessary evil, but sleeping with her would pretty much purchase him a one-way ticket to hell. Because if she was innocent, he would have slept with a woman while lying about who he was. A woman who'd already been used by one liar. And if she was guilty, he'd have to live with the knowledge that he'd had sex with the woman helping Russ's murderer.

He let himself in through the front door and went upstairs, where he found AJ in the master bedroom, manning the monitors.

The second Caleb entered the room, AJ let out a hoot, followed by a round of applause. "I'm thoroughly impressed," his partner drawled. "You move fast, man."

Caleb smothered a groan. He'd been hoping AJ hadn't seen the kiss, but from the lewd way the man wiggled his eyebrows, he'd obviously caught the show.

"I was trying to distract her," Caleb muttered.

"With your tongue? You could have just asked for a tour of the house."

Caleb ignored the remark and said, "Aside from climbing trees, did you do anything productive today? Any headway on where the wire transfer came from?"

"Still nothing." AJ leaned back in the chair. "But I'm close, and I can tell you, the money wasn't wired from the States. I traced it to Europe. Not sure which country, though."

Europe, huh? It made sense, if the money that had appeared in the account was being used to fund Grier's way out of the country.

"What if Grier tries to move the money?" he asked, a frown puckering his brow.

"He can't," AJ answered, looking smug. "We set it up so that money can come in—that way we can track it—but Grier and Kincaid can't move the money out. I hope they try, though. I'd love to be a fly on the wall when they realize the hundred Gs is stuck there."

They. The word hung in Caleb's mind like a black rain cloud. AJ still hadn't ruled Marley out as a suspect, and it was beginning to bother him. After these last couple of encounters with Marley, he was less suspicious of her than ever. Caleb's instincts continued to tell him Marley wasn't helping Grier, but he knew he couldn't rule it out entirely. Still, it grated a little, hearing AJ lump her into Grier's villainous category.

"What about you?" AJ asked. "Aside from playing tonsil hockey with the nurse, what'd you find out?"

"Nothing," Caleb said with a sigh.

Not entirely true, of course. He'd found out plenty of things. Like how sweet she tasted. How pliant and welcoming her lips were. How hot her skin felt beneath his fingers.

"You mean your overwhelming charisma didn't win her over?"

Caleb bristled. "I offered to help her paint tomorrow, so maybe we'll get lucky and she'll open up then."

AJ's black eyes narrowed. "And what about you?"

"What do you mean?"

"Will *you* be getting lucky?"

The sudden bite to AJ's tone was unexpected. Caleb met his partner's wary gaze head-on. "Come on, AJ, I told you I'm not going to sleep with her."

"You sure? Because that make-out session looked pretty damn hot. Actually, it looked like you were going to beat your chest a couple of times, throw her over your shoulder and drag her upstairs so you could screw her brains out."

Caleb's lips tightened. "I was playing a part. I have no intention of taking her to bed."

"Uh-huh…"

"For the love of—"

"How long has it been since you got laid?"

Caleb's eyes flashed. "That has nothing to do with anything."

"No? I think it has a lot to do with this. Look, I get it. She's an attractive woman. But don't—"

"Don't what?" Caleb cut in. "Forget why I'm here?"

"I'm just asking you to be careful. Grier needs to be behind bars for what he did to Russ. And I can't have a cute blonde distracting you from catching him if he shows up."

"She won't. Trust me, I want Grier as much as you

do." Caleb swallowed. "Russ was the best friend I ever had, damn it. And tomorrow I plan on getting the truth out of Marley. If she knows anything, I'll find out, okay?"

AJ looked unconvinced. "And if she suddenly rips all her clothes off and begs you to do nasty things to her?"

Caleb swallowed harder, forcing himself not to imagine the ridiculously tempting scenario AJ had just described. "Then I say no," he maintained. "I'm serious, man. I'm not going to sleep with her."

"And if she unrolls the yoga mat and starts doing naked pelvic thrusts…"

He gritted his teeth. "I'm *not* going to sleep with her."

But oh, how he wanted to.

Not gonna happen, man.

No, he wouldn't let it happen. The weeklong attraction he'd felt for Marley might have culminated in an explosive kiss, but he was determined not to let it go further.

He just hoped he had the strength.

Scratch that—he *prayed* he had the strength.

MARLEY WAS WIDE AWAKE and dressed for manual labor when the doorbell rang the next afternoon. She'd taken a power nap when she got home from the hospital, and her alert state was actually a bit of a surprise. There had been a massive car accident on Interstate 5 and half the nurses from the respiratory unit where Marley usually worked had been reassigned to the E.R. for a couple of days to tend to the onslaught of victims. Marley was one of them, and she'd been running around like a chicken with its head cut off for the past nine hours.

Yet here she was, bright-eyed and ready to paint her kitchen. Figure that one out.

Okay, well, maybe it wasn't that hard to comprehend, considering who she would be painting the kitchen with.

She opened the door and there he was, wearing a pair of faded blue jeans and a black T-shirt. The shirt clung to his muscular chest, a sight that made Marley's heart race like a Formula One car. Darn it, why did he have to be so attractive?

And why had she let him kiss her? They'd only just met, for Pete's sake. Only a couple days ago she'd been telling Gwen she wanted to take things slow when it came to her love life, that getting intimate with a stranger scared her. And what had she done? Gotten intimate with a stranger.

"Hey," Caleb greeted her. His deep voice had a sexy rasp that brought a rush of heat to Marley's belly. "Ready to paint?"

She gestured for him to come in. "Ready, yes. Excited about it, no."

His lips quirked and she instantly focused on his sensual mouth. Her legs trembled as she thought about the kiss they'd shared. The memory of Caleb's warm mouth and skillful tongue ignited a charge of heat through her body, hot little flames that licked at her skin.

"Tough day at work?" he asked as he followed her inside.

"Very tough," she admitted. "I was assigned to the E.R. because there was a huge accident this morning. A tour bus taking twenty people to a casino collided with an eighteen-wheeler."

"I saw it on the news. Was it as bad as it looked?" Caleb asked.

"Worse. Seven dead, twelve injured." She led him into the kitchen, where she'd already set up all the paint trays and rollers they'd need.

"How do you do it?" His voice was low and laced with awe. "How can you look at so much death and carnage day in and day out?"

"I like helping people," she said simply.

He didn't respond, and when she looked over, she noticed him watching her with some expression she couldn't quite decipher. Admiration? Or was it curiosity?

She cleared her throat and picked up the large paint can labeled Morning Sunshine. "Um, so, you can start on that wall," she said, pointing to the wall opposite the back door. She moved her hand toward the adjacent wall, adding, "I still need to get rid of the rest of the wallpaper on this one, and then we can prime it."

"Yes, ma'am." A glint of humor filled his eyes, but his face remained as stoic as usual.

She wondered why he smiled so rarely. Difficult childhood, or was he just serious by nature? She didn't mind, though. She'd faked enough smiles these past few months that it was refreshing not having to put on a happy face to avoid being on the receiving end of the sympathetic smiles she'd grown used to.

It was even more refreshing not having to make awkward small talk, which she discovered ten minutes later as they worked in comfortable silence. Caleb didn't say much, except for the occasional work-related remark, as he rolled bright-yellow paint on her kitchen wall.

She found herself sneaking sidelong glances in his

direction, admiring his perfect profile, the strength of his jaw, the confident way he moved. Her pulse sped up each time he lifted his arms, which made his powerful muscles bunch and flex. His body was incredible, hard and lean without an ounce of fat. And she loved how focused he was on his task, his head bent in concentration. As he painted, a rogue lock of dark hair fell onto his forehead. She wanted to walk over and brush it away, but kept her hands on the scraper she was using. Just because every nerve ending in her body crackled with the need to touch him didn't mean she'd give in to temptation.

She forced herself to keep working, succeeding in removing nearly all the wallpaper before her parched throat finally got the best of her. "How about a break?" she suggested.

Caleb glanced over with a slight grin. "We've only been at this for an hour. I thought you were tougher than that, Kincaid."

A tiny alarm went off in her head. Had she told him her last name? She couldn't remember, but she didn't think so. Or maybe…the mailbox, she deduced with relief. He must have seen her last name on the mailbox.

"I'm also thirsty," she retorted.

"And you had a long night," he added in concession. "So I'm willing to overlook your laziness."

Rolling her eyes, she headed for the fridge. "Iced tea okay?"

"Yep."

She poured two tall glasses, then grabbed a few ice cubes from the freezer. Caleb was sitting at the table when she came back, rolling his shoulders in a way that made his pecs flex against his shirt. Her dry mouth went even dryer.

She sat down, sipping her drink and hoping the cold liquid would ease the fire inside her. Silence hung in the kitchen again, only this time it made her feel awkward. God, it was strange having a man here. Three months ago, it had been Patrick in Caleb's chair, reading the paper and eating the scrambled eggs she used to make him.

Her chest squeezed with anger. Though she tried masking the shot of pain that streaked through her, Caleb evidently sensed it.

"Are you okay?" he asked.

Marley put down her cup. "I'm fine." Her stomach burned, and she tried to control the volatile reaction thoughts of Patrick evoked inside her. "I was just thinking about something…someone… Don't worry about it."

"Anyone important?"

She couldn't help a harsh laugh. "You could say that."

A knowing glimmer filled his blue eyes. "An ex?"

She nodded.

"How long ago did you break up?"

He sounded curious, but not pushy, and something about his tone compelled her to answer. "It's been a few months now." She sighed. "And let's just say it didn't end well."

"I'm sorry."

That was it. *I'm sorry.* Marley suddenly felt like hugging him. Everyone she knew, when they'd heard about Patrick, had grilled her about the breakup. Even her dad, God bless him, wanted to know everything— as if hearing every last detail could somehow help him protect her after the fact. But Caleb didn't dig, he didn't pry or demand, and for that reason, she found herself revealing things she would never usually tell a stranger.

"He wasn't the person I thought he was." She wrapped her fingers around the cold glass, needing to hold on to something. "He lied to me about everything, starting with who he really was."

Caleb's face remained expressionless, but she saw a muscle twitch in his jaw. "He sounds like a pretty awful guy."

"Big time." Her hand trembled. "I still want to kick myself for ever falling in love with him."

To her surprise, the sympathy she expected to see wasn't there. Instead, he just shrugged and, in a rough voice, said, "You can't always help who you fall for. Or at least that's what I've heard."

Marley studied his face. "Heard, not felt, huh?" She took a chance and decided to venture into dangerous territory. "So you've never been in love?"

CALEB WASN'T PREPARED FOR the question, but he knew he'd opened this can of worms by asking her about Grier. And the answers she'd given perplexed him. His gut still told him she wasn't helping Grier, that she hadn't known a thing about Grier's crimes. So why wasn't she angrier? Hell hath no fury like a woman scorned, right?

When she'd spoken of Grier just now, Caleb had only seen pain and bitterness in her eyes. Not the fury *he'd* be feeling if someone close had deceived him. Marley, though…she simply looked sad.

"Caleb?"

Her melodic voice drew him from his thoughts. He tried to remember what she'd asked him, but the sight of her was far too distracting. Her lips, pink and lush, looked so utterly kissable, and her hair was coming out of its ponytail again, loose blond waves falling forward in the most appealing way.

He curled his hand around his iced-tea glass. He had to quit getting distracted by her curvy body and beautiful face. What had she asked again? Oh, yeah, love...

"No," he said grudgingly. "I can't say I've ever been in love."

Curiosity and surprise pooled in her big brown eyes. "How old are you?"

"Thirty-one."

"And you've really never been in love?"

He focused on his drink, raising it to his lips and taking a long sip, delaying his response. Why did she look so bewildered? Lots of people had never been in love, right?

"It just hasn't happened to me," he said. "And you know what? Half the time I think that's a good thing. Seems like love ends in disaster more often than not."

"It does," she agreed.

"But you haven't given up?"

She leaned back in her chair, the action causing her breasts to jut enticingly against the material of her yellow tank top. Caleb forced himself to look only at her face. Anything lower than that was guaranteed to blow his concentration to smithereens.

"No, I haven't given up," she said in a soft voice. "Sure, I might have some trust issues now, thanks to my ex, but I'm working through those. You know, trying to understand why I didn't see the signs, why I let him manipulate me so completely. But I still think love can be a good thing, if you find the right person."

Caleb absorbed everything she'd just said. Love. It

was such a foreign concept to him, since growing up he hadn't had any of it. He'd never known his father, and his mother had decided drugs were more important than her five-year-old son. In a sense, his first relationship with a woman ended up with him finding his mom's overdosed body on the living-room carpet.

Could love be a good thing? To him, the answer was a big fat no. What was the point in opening yourself up to another person when they would only kick you aside sooner or later?

He scraped back his chair, discomfort gathering in his gut. This was too…intimate. He was getting too close to sharing a very private part of himself with this woman, and he couldn't do that. It made him uneasy.

"We should get back to work," he said.

Marley nodded. "I'm almost done with the wallpaper," she replied, getting up to drag a small stepladder toward the wall. She climbed up on it, looking over at him and adding, "I just need to finish this part near the ceiling and then we can—" A yelp flew out of her mouth as she lost her balance.

Caleb reacted instantly, reaching the spot just in time for her to topple right into his arms. A flash of heat tore through his body as he found himself yet again cupping her firm bottom. His groin stirred and hardened. Her sweet scent assaulted him, mingling with the paint fumes in the air and making him light-headed with desire.

"What is it with you and ladders?" he asked roughly.

She stared up at him, amusement dancing in her eyes. "I never claimed to be graceful, okay?"

He choked back a laugh. "Good, because you're not."

They stared at each other for a moment and

something in the air shifted. She had one arm around his shoulder, the other pressed against his chest and her touch seared through the material of his shirt and heated his flesh. The room grew thick with tension, heavy with attraction. He wanted to taste her again. To drag his hands over that exquisite body, kiss her, touch her, until she cried out with pleasure.

Suddenly he couldn't move, couldn't breathe. He knew he should let her down, but his arms refused to cooperate. They just held her tighter, pulled her closer.

"Um, so..." Her voice came out husky. She stopped talking, the tip of her tongue darting out to moisten her lips.

"Don't do that," he burst out.

She froze. "Do what?"

"Lick your lips like that." Despite himself, he reached out to rub the bare flesh of her arm.

Marley's breath hitched. "Why not?"

He ran his hand up and down her hot skin. "Because it's already hard enough."

"What's hard enough?" she whispered.

"Trying not to kiss you again."

Those big brown eyes glimmered with heat. His cock swelled as her gaze moved to his mouth. For God's sake, didn't she realize he only wanted to kiss her more when she looked at him like that?

"You know what I think?" she said, her soft voice sliding over him like a sensual caress.

"What?"

She rubbed her palm against his chest in a feather-light stroke, then twined both arms around his neck and murmured, "I think you should just go for it."

With her head slanted up toward him and her lush

lips pursed, Caleb knew there was no way he could resist her. He wanted this. No, he *needed* this.

He slowly lowered his head. Their lips were inches apart, so close. Not close enough. An unsteady breath left his mouth. He shouldn't do this. His lips moved closer, nearly touching hers. He really, really shouldn't do—

A loud chime rang through the kitchen, startling them both. Their heads moved apart, and Caleb nearly lost his grip on the sexy woman in his arms.

"An email just came in," she murmured in explanation.

The annoying chime sounded again, and Caleb traced it to the open laptop sitting on the counter.

"Ignore it," she said, sounding a little breathless. "It's probably just my brother. He's supposed to send me pictures of tiles."

But the moment had passed, and the interruption had been much needed. Saved by email. Caleb's entire body shrieked in protest as he gently set Marley on her feet. His pulse was still racing, his cock stiffer than a two-by-four, but he knew his body would forgive him. He wasn't sure he'd be able to forgive himself if things went any further.

He was lying to her about who he was, for God's sake. Getting involved with Marley would be a terrible mistake. Not to mention unbelievably callous.

"You should check it," he said, taking a step backward.

The disappointment flashing across her face tore at him. *You don't want me,* he wanted to tell her. *You don't know me.* But he kept his mouth shut, and after a moment, she walked over to the counter.

He used the distance between them to collect his

composure, to steady himself and will away his massive erection. Marley was bent over the laptop, clicking away. She waited for a page to load, clicked again and then all the color rapidly drained from her face.

"Everything okay?" he called warily.

She didn't answer. Just remained glued to the screen, her face growing impossibly paler.

"Oh, my God," she whispered.

Caleb took brisk strides toward the counter, but Marley was shielding the computer screen from his view. "What's going on?" he demanded.

Slowly, she lifted her head and looked at him. The terror and confusion he saw in her gaze raised every warning flag he had.

"It's him." She shuddered. "Why won't he leave me alone? Why can't he just—" Her breath was quick and shallow. "Oh, God. I have to call the police."

5

"MARLEY, YOU NEED TO CALM DOWN and tell me what's going on," Caleb said in a firm tone.

But she was already marching over to the phone, mumbling unintelligible things. As she dialed, Caleb leaned forward to examine the page on the laptop, the message that had just shaken Marley's entire world. He hissed in a breath as he read the words on the screen.

I miss you, sweet pea. Stay strong. I'll see you soon.

Caleb's body hardened with icy fury. Grier. That son of a bitch had contacted Marley, just as Caleb had known he would.

"Detective Hernandez," he heard Marley stammer from behind him. "Yes…please…tell him it's urgent."

Caleb read Grier's message again. Short, but sweet. Each word was branded into his brain, the last four bringing a wave of satisfaction and a jolt of adrenaline. Grier was coming for her. Caleb had known Grier wouldn't be able to stay away. Yet along with the gratification of knowing that his hunch had been right, a knot of fear twined around his insides as he realized precisely how much danger Marley was in.

Grier's saccharine words rang of love, not hate, but when you were dealing with sociopaths there wasn't always a clear line between the two. Grier could turn on Marley any second. Hell, he could decide to strangle her to death if he didn't like the way she prepared his coffee. The knowledge of what had happened to the last woman Grier was involved with wasn't lost on Caleb. They'd never been able to conclusively tie him to her murder, but the circumstantial evidence was overwhelming. With nothing concrete to charge him with, the case had gone cold. Still, everyone involved felt Grier was their man.

Shit. He needed to call his supervisor and arrange for more agents to watch Marley, maybe get the local cops to patrol the neighborhood. Even Hernandez would have to agree this email spelled danger.

Hernandez. Damn. Marley was speaking to him at this very moment, her voice shaky as she told him about the message.

He had to get out of here. And fast. The local police detective knew about the stakeout, but not that Caleb had made contact. Which meant that his cover could be blown the moment the detective walked into the house and saw Caleb there.

"The detective in charge of the case is on his way over."

Marley's voice pulled him from his panicked thoughts. He turned to face her, glad to see some color returning to her face.

She gave him a rueful look. "I guess I have some explaining to do, huh?"

Caleb faltered. Explaining? Why would she need to—because he wasn't supposed to know about any of this... She wasn't aware that he knew about Grier, that he'd been hunting the guy for three months. That his best friend and partner had been killed because of her ex.

"Yeah," he said, finding his voice. "That might be helpful." He gestured to the laptop. "I'm sorry, I read the email. You were so upset, and I wanted to see—"

"It's fine," she interrupted. "Come on, let's sit."

He followed her back to the table, but even after they were seated, Marley didn't continue. She suddenly seemed lost, turmoil and anger roiling in her brown eyes.

"Who was the message from?" he asked.

"My ex," she said flatly. "Who made it pretty clear he's coming after me."

"I'm afraid I don't quite understand."

She inhaled slowly. "Remember I told you he wasn't who he said he was? Well, what I found out that he was a drug dealer."

Without preamble, she told him everything. She skimmed over the romance, but spoke in detail about the day she'd found out from the police who Patrick was, the investigation that followed, the shame and horror she'd felt when she learned the truth.

Each word made his temples throb. The disbelief dripping from her voice was unmistakable. So was the disgust in her eyes. AJ was wrong. There was now no doubt in Caleb's mind that Marley had been completely ignorant of her fiancé's criminal dealings.

Nobody could act that well. Nobody could fake the horror conveyed in each word she spoke.

"And now he emails me?" she finished, looking at him with wide eyes. "God, Caleb, what if he shows up here?"

Then I'll catch him.

He bit back the words, instead leaning forward in the chair and resting his elbows on the table. "I'm sure the police will do everything they can to protect you, Marley. They won't just let a murderer waltz into your home."

"Hernandez might," she said bitterly. "That man hates me. He thinks I knew about Patrick all along and that I'm somehow helping him now."

"Why the heck would he think that?"

"I don't know." She shook her head in anger. "He has it in for me, and I've never done a single thing to the man. And now he's coming over, and he'll probably grill me again and accuse me of sending the email myself."

Caleb stifled a sigh. Yeah, with Hernandez, some grilling would definitely be involved. He didn't understand what Hernandez had against Marley, but he made a mental note to ask AJ to get his hands on the detective's file. Caleb couldn't afford to lose Grier because of some stupid vendetta.

"Maybe he'll be more receptive this time," Caleb said, trying to sound positive. "He must be getting anxious, trying to find your ex, and this could be a big break in the case."

Marley didn't look convinced. "Will you stay while he questions me? I know this doesn't really involve you, but…" She exhaled. "I'd feel better if I had someone on my side for this."

How on earth was he supposed to say no to that?

Reluctance welled up in his chest. He couldn't stick around. Hernandez might slip up when he saw him, do something dim-witted like call Caleb "Agent Ford." If Marley found out who he really was, she would be furious. Most likely she'd throw him out and refuse to have any further contact with him. Then again, she was an intelligent woman; she might see the benefit of having a cop close by.

But he couldn't take the chance that fury might cloud her judgment. AJ had persuaded him to befriend Marley so he could gain information, but now that Grier had contacted her, Caleb had an even more important reason to stay by her side. He'd never be able to forgive himself if Grier hurt Marley—if he killed her, the way he'd killed Russ.

Caleb's blood pressure spiked. Marley was still waiting for his answer, and for the life of him, he couldn't leave her right now. "Let's sit in the living room," he said with a small sigh.

They walked into the spacious room, which contained a comfortable brown couch, a huge bookshelf crammed with novels, and a large window overlooking the front yard. As Marley sank down onto the couch, Caleb went to the window, fixing his gaze on the driveway.

How was he going to get out of this? Detective Hernandez would arrive any freaking second. Caleb needed to intercept the man before he entered the house.

Behind him, Marley sat with her back ramrod

straight. Caleb wanted nothing more than to draw her into his arms and offer words of comfort, but he couldn't. Not until he figured out how to get Hernandez alone before the man questioned Marley.

Tension coiled into a tight knot in his gut as he spotted an unmarked black sedan pulling into the driveway. He started for the front door. Marley followed him, but he placed a hand on her arm before she could reach for the doorknob.

"I want to go out there and talk to him first," he said.

She blinked. "Why?"

"To make a few things clear to him before he comes in here and starts treating you like a suspect," he improvised.

"Caleb, don't—"

Before she could object further, he darted out the door and descended the porch just as Hernandez stepped onto Marley's driveway. The detective was short and stocky, with a head of black hair streaked with gray, and dark eyes that widened at the sight of Caleb. "Agent Ford?" Hernandez said.

Caleb closed the distance between them, glad the detective hadn't spoken any louder. "Hey, Miguel."

Hernandez's thick black mustache curled as he drew his lips together in a frown. "What the hell are you doing in there with her? I thought Stevens had you next door."

"He does, but I had to make contact."

Hernandez looked suspicious. "Why?"

"It was necessary. Look, I'm undercover, Miguel. Kincaid thinks I'm her writer neighbor, and I need her to keep thinking that."

The detective's frown deepened. "The department still views her as a suspect, Ford."

"The department might need to change that opinion then," he retorted. "I don't believe Kincaid had any knowledge of her fiancé's previous or current crimes. But I do believe Grier will contact her again, especially after the message he sent twenty minutes ago."

"The email she *claims* he sent," Hernandez said.

"It's real, Miguel. And before we go in there, I need your word that you'll maintain my cover. We don't know each other."

Hernandez paused for a moment, looking both intrigued and wary. "We don't know each other," he finally agreed.

The two men crossed Marley's lawn and climbed the porch. Marley was waiting at the door. The moment she saw Hernandez, her delicate mouth tightened in a thin line. "Detective Hernandez," she said coolly, casting Caleb a suspicious look.

"Ms. Kincaid." Hernandez's nod of greeting was polite, but it was still obvious how he felt about Marley. He didn't trust her.

"Let's go into the kitchen," Caleb suggested.

Unable to stop himself, he placed a possessive hand on the small of Marley's back, ignored the slight raise of Hernandez's fuzzy black eyebrows and headed for the kitchen.

MARLEY HAD TROUBLE CONTAINING her distaste as she watched Hernandez read the email. He'd slipped on a pair of latex gloves before handling the laptop, as if he expected Patrick's fingerprints to be on it or something. Right, because she'd secretly met up with Patrick, let him use her computer so he could send her an email and then come home and called the police. Why did this man distrust her so much? She'd never been in trouble with the law, didn't even have any outstanding parking tickets and yet here he was, treating her like a common criminal.

"Has anyone had access to this laptop other than the two of you?" Hernandez asked.

"No," Marley replied. "I'm the only one who uses it."

He stared at the screen again. "Do you recognize the email address the message came from?"

"No. Patrick's address was the one on his domain name, for his web design company."

"He most likely used one of those free email accounts," Caleb spoke up, leaning against the counter. "He probably went to an internet café to do it."

"Maybe," the detective said, "but that's for us to figure out. Why don't you focus on—what is it you do, Mr. Ford? Writer?"

She noticed a muscle twitch in Caleb's jaw. "Yes," he muttered.

"Then focus on writing and let us do our job."

The detective's voice was so cold most people probably would've cowered and shut up, but not Caleb. To Marley's amazement, he crossed his arms over his spectacular chest and said, "I'm sure you have a bunch of tech guys at the station who can locate the IP address of the computer the message was sent on. But what about Marley? I assume you'll assign some officers to protect her."

The detective spared a pithy look in Marley's direction. "I'm afraid we don't have the budget for that."

Barely contained anger seethed in Caleb's blue eyes.

"Come on, Detective, you read the note. He's obviously planning to make a move soon. I was under the impression you've been searching for this guy for some time."

"We have been." Hernandez let out a resigned breath. To Marley's surprise, he caved in to Caleb's request. "I'll arrange some patrols around the neighborhood and talk to the captain about posting an officer outside the house."

Marley glanced from Caleb to Hernandez. There was a strange ripple of tension between them, and neither man seemed to like the other very much. She understood, at least from Caleb's perspective. She hadn't liked Hernandez from the moment they'd met. What she did like, however, was how Caleb didn't even flinch as he met the other man's gaze head-on.

A tiny thrill shot through her. She needed to stop being so closed off and suspicious. It actually felt nice, having someone in her corner.

"I'm going to have to confiscate the computer," Hernandez said, his words sounding stilted. He picked up the laptop and tucked it under his arm. "The boys at the station will try to figure out where the email came from."

"Thank you," Marley said.

Hernandez slowly studied her face. "Is this the first contact Grier has made?"

She nodded.

"Are you sure about that?"

Marley's spine stiffened. She opened her mouth to reply, but Caleb spoke before she could. "Why do you insist on treating her like a suspect?" he asked in an even voice.

"I'm doing my job, Mr. Ford. I'm expected to examine every angle."

"Well, you're wasting your time on this one. Marley didn't do anything wrong. She was used and lied to, and you might actually get a break in the case if you focused your attention on more important *angles*."

Hernandez looked absolutely livid. The tension in the kitchen skyrocketed, mingling with the rage radiating from both men. Marley sighed and quickly attempted to diffuse their volatile emotions.

"This is the first time Patrick has contacted me," she said loudly. "And yes, I'm sure. As I told you three months ago, Patrick went to a design convention and never came back. Two days later, you showed up at my door and told me who he really is. And a half hour ago, he emailed me. That's all I can tell you, Detective."

"Okay, then. We'll get on this email development right away." Scowling at Caleb, Hernandez took a step toward the doorway. "And if he tries to make contact again, call us immediately."

Nodding, Marley led the detective out of her kitchen and walked him to the front door. Caleb trailed behind them, his shoulders stiff. She offered Hernandez a polite thank-you for his help, then leaned against the door frame and watched as he strode to his car with her laptop under his arm.

The engine of the black sedan roared to life, and then Hernandez drove off. Marley turned to face Caleb. "I appreciate your sticking up for me like that, but I don't know if it was a good idea for you to interfere with Hernandez."

She still couldn't believe he'd done it. He didn't even know her, yet he'd reprimanded the detective, the conviction in his voice so strong when he'd insisted she couldn't be helping Patrick.

"He'll get over it," Caleb said, shrugging.

"You're a good man, Caleb. Not many people would defend someone they've only known a few days. For all you know, I really could be helping Patrick."

"You wouldn't do that," he said, sounding gruff.

Despite her reservations emotion filled her chest, making Marley's throat tighten. His faith in her came as an odd relief. She normally didn't care what people thought. As long as her family and close friends knew what kind of person she was, it didn't matter what jerks like Hernandez believed. But knowing that Caleb trusted her brought an unexpected rush of pleasure.

She realized she was starting to like him a lot. Not just because he'd caught her when she'd fallen off the roof or because he'd offered to help her renovate. There was something about his quiet strength and rare laughter that made her heart jump. She was shocked at how quickly her feelings were growing.

"I have to go," he said, then cleared his throat. "I'm next door if you need me. If anything happens, if your ex causes any trouble, don't hesitate to come and get me, okay? Day or night, Marley."

All she could do was nod, amazed by the sincerity in his deep voice. He really meant it. He would actually be willing to protect her, a woman he'd just met. Maybe there *were* some good and decent men left in this world.

As his hand reached for the doorknob, she burst out, "Wait."

Caleb turned. "Yeah?"

Without another word, she eliminated the distance

between them, cupped his strong jaw with both hands, and kissed him.

Like placing a hand on a hot stove, her body got an immediate reaction from the feel of his firm lips against hers. Heat torpedoed into her, and she deepened the kiss, needing to taste him. He hesitated when she ran her tongue along the seam of his lips, seeking entry, but then he let her in.

She flicked her tongue over his, eliciting a ragged groan from deep in his throat. He was restraining himself, and she didn't like it. So she pressed her body closer to his and wrapped her arms around him. Feeling bold, she let her hands skim down his body to touch his taut ass. Gave it a little squeeze, too.

Caleb chuckled against her mouth. "Did you just squeeze my butt?"

"Mmm-hmm." She brushed her lips over his. "Are you complaining?" Without letting him reply, she kissed him again. Caleb was so darn reserved all the time. She wanted to see some of his control crumble, wanted to feel him let go.

She got her wish seconds later, when he suddenly released a husky growl and returned the kiss with fervor. And then he was touching her, his warm hands stroking her hips, caressing her belly, reaching around to cup her bottom. He squeezed her the way she'd just done to him, then moved his hands back to her waist and began to drag his palms over her stomach, slowly traveling up to her breasts.

Her nipples pebbled, her core burning with passion. Marley shivered, whimpered, then gasped when he grazed the underside of each breast. God, she wanted him to touch her. To fondle her and kiss her and slide into her—

He abruptly broke off the kiss, his hands dropping from her chest. "I should go." Each word was a hoarse gasp.

Marley was still a little stunned, amazed by her own boldness, but even more surprised by the sparks crackling between them like fireworks. She wanted him so badly every inch of her body ached and tingled. What was happening to her?

"Will you have dinner with me tomorrow night?" she asked impulsively. "My treat."

He ran one hand through his scruffy hair, drawing her attention to the fleck of yellow paint caught in his dark tresses. "No painting involved," she added, grinning.

Hesitation flickered across his face. "I don't know, I have a lot of work to do."

"Please?" She swallowed. "I could use the company."

She knew he was thinking about the email her psychotic ex-fiancé had just sent her—she was thinking about it, too. When he finally nodded, pleasure bloomed inside her.

"Okay," he agreed. "What time?"

"I'll be home from the hospital around five, so how's seven?"

"Seven," he confirmed.

She opened the door for him, smiling. "I'll see you tomorrow then."

Caleb gave a slight nod, bade her goodbye and stepped onto the porch. She watched him walk off, then closed her front door and went back inside.

Her heart did a little jumping jack, and not even the memory of Patrick's disgustingly loving email could bring down her mood. The police would find Patrick. She had to believe in that, otherwise she'd be cowering in fear, hiding in her bedroom closet or something. No matter how apprehensive the thought of Patrick coming back here made her, she wasn't going to cower. She was stronger than that.

And right now, all she wanted to do was bask in the surprising and delicious feelings Caleb inspired in her and look forward to sharing dinner with a man who wasn't a psychotic criminal.

"Son of a bitch," Patrick muttered under his breath, his eyes glued to the dark-haired man who'd just walked out of Marley's house.

Anger bubbled in Patrick's gut as he noticed the other man's cocky stride. The guy walked like a cop.

Probably because he was one.

Patrick's entire body had turned into a block of ice when he'd seen that unmarked cruiser slide into Marley's driveway, but the shock hadn't been as great as the one he'd experienced when a very familiar DEA agent strolled outside to exchange a few words with the detective.

He clenched his fists. He'd known the cops were watching Marley, but the DEA had someone right next door? Shit. That would make getting to her a hell of a lot more difficult.

Did she know her neighbor was a cop? Patrick froze as he pondered that question. No, the agent must be pulling the wool over her eyes. Marley would never work with the cops. She was on *his* side.

Then why did she give the fat detective her laptop?

"They were tracking her email," he mumbled after a moment. He'd thought about that when he was at the internet café sending her the message, but he'd figured it was a risk he could afford to take. The cops would trace the email to the computer at the café, but it wasn't like Patrick would be hanging around there, sipping lattes.

Marley had no choice. She'd had to give them her computer. What worried him more was the disconcerting presence of the agent next door. Patrick remembered him from the raid. The bastard had pointed a gun at him, ordered him to surrender. And now here he was, waiting for another chance to make his arrest.

"They won't catch me," Patrick said smugly, turning his attention to the woman on the bed.

He'd moved Lydia out of the closet to give her a little bit of air—he wasn't a monster, after all—but she was still bound and gagged. Still looking at him with those terrified eyes.

"Relax," he said with a sigh. "I'm not going to hurt you. I already told you that."

She whimpered, bringing a wave of irritation to his gut. Striding over to the bed, he sat down on the edge and stared directly at her. "I'm not a bad guy, all right? So quit looking at me like that. What's so wrong with wanting to make a little money?"

The old lady couldn't answer because of the gag stretched across her mouth, but the look in her eyes was annoyingly familiar. His parents used to sport that same expression, when he told them about all the big plans he had for himself. They didn't understand, though. His parents were too bland, too ordinary. They were perfectly happy living in their crappy little Iowa town, teaching math to snot-faced schoolchildren, and letting their lives pass them by.

Well, Patrick wasn't like them. All he'd ever wished for as a child was to get out of Nowhereville, Iowa, and *be* somebody. He wanted to live life. He wanted millions of dollars in the bank and yachts and trips around the world.

But above all that, he wanted Marley.

She was beautiful and kind and good. And a bad boy like him needed a good girl like her for balance.

Except now he had that asshole cop to contend with. It would be no easy feat, getting the money he'd stashed under the tile in Marley's bathroom, but he knew he'd find a way.

He always did, after all.

6

CALEB SPENT MOST of the morning going over his files on Patrick Grier, focusing on the list of known associates and persons of interest, and trying to figure out who Grier might turn to for help other than his ex-fiancée. By the early afternoon he gave up. The DEA and local law enforcement had already scoured that list for months, and so far it hadn't produced any leads. There was some hope with a former contact of Grier's in Mexico, but the man wasn't talking and no amount of pressure seemed to help.

Getting up from his chair, Caleb rubbed his eyes, then glanced at the bed, noticing that all the sheets lay in a tangled mess on the floor. He'd been awake most of the night, tossing, turning, cursing and trying not to think about Marley. Of course, he'd failed miserably, and in the end he'd been up for hours, tossing, turning, cursing and *totally* thinking about Marley.

He'd contemplated going to the guest room next door and dragging AJ out of bed, maybe getting a game of poker going, but he'd resisted the urge. AJ wouldn't understand the feelings Caleb was developing for Marley.

Disturbing feelings. His emotions, normally tightly reined in, now flowed like water from a leaky faucet, and he was helpless to turn them off.

He liked Marley.

No, he *really* liked her. And he wanted her so badly he couldn't think straight anymore. Just the thought of her made every part of his body ache. His head. His groin. His heart.

"Forget about that," he mumbled to himself, raking his fingers through his hair as he leaned back. "Focus on the job."

Unfortunately, his body wouldn't let him forget. He had an erection of colossal proportions straining against the front of his gray sweatpants, and in his groin an ache so deep his bones hurt.

His cell phone started ringing before he could slink off to the bathroom and resort to self-gratification. Noticing the caller ID, he suppressed a sigh and picked up the phone.

"Hello, sir," he said.

A vile curse battered his eardrums. "What's going on over there, Ford?" his supervisor demanded.

"What do you mean?"

Ken Stevens wasn't put off by his casual tone. "Miguel Hernandez just gave me a call, wanting to know why one of my agents is cozying up to Marley Kincaid."

Thanks a lot, Hernandez.

"I'm not cozying up to her," he replied. "I had no choice but to make contact with her." Quickly, he explained the ladder incident, finishing with, "AJ thought since I'd already interacted with her, I should keep it up to see if she knows anything about Grier."

"And does she?"

"No."

Stevens made a frustrated noise. "Next time, speak to me before you decide to go against protocol." Stevens paused. "What's this email Hernandez mentioned?"

Caleb told him what the message contained, even though Stevens probably had a copy of it sitting in front of him on his desk. "I told you he wouldn't be able to stay away from her," he said. "He's going to make a move soon, sir. I feel it in my gut."

"Then stay put and keep your eyes open."

Despite his sometimes hotheaded nature, Stevens had always possessed a great deal of faith in Caleb and his abilities, which Caleb appreciated at the moment. He knew his boss wasn't happy that he'd befriended Marley, but both men understood that there were bigger things to worry about at the moment.

"I'll catch him, sir," Caleb said "He's been lucky all these years, keeping his cover solid, avoiding charges, but his luck is up. I think he's obsessed with Kincaid, and he will come for her."

Stevens sighed. "He'd better."

"No breaks on your end?"

"Lukas is still monitoring the bank account Grier opened with Kincaid, but there haven't been any more deposits and no withdrawal attempts. I've got six agents on the airports, two watching San Diego General and a few more talking to Grier's associates. We're running out of manpower."

Stevens's voice hardened. "Don't get too close to her, Ford. Keep the contact casual—we can't risk having this case thrown out of court if you get involved with a witness. And keep me posted."

As usual, his supervisor hung up without uttering

a goodbye. Stevens didn't have time for pleasantries, never had.

Caleb set the phone on the desk and glanced down at his ratty sweatpants, then lifted his hand to his chin and rubbed the thick stubble he hadn't bothered to shave this morning. He should, though. He couldn't have dinner with Marley looking like a disheveled lumberjack.

He rubbed his forehead, wondering what the hell he'd gotten himself into. His job at the agency was all he had, all he cared about, and here he was, risking it for a woman with big brown eyes and a gorgeous smile.

Why couldn't he stay away from her? He had no reason to maintain contact—he was already convinced she had no information about Grier. He should be walking away from her, not running straight toward her.

He could always cancel their dinner date. Tell her he was sick or that he had to go out of town. But then he imagined the disappointment in her voice when he backed out, and knew he couldn't do it. He didn't want to disappoint Marley. He wished he knew where these protective instincts had sprung from and why he so desperately wanted to make her happy.

Don't get too close to her.

He almost laughed. What would Stevens do if he knew Caleb was going over there tonight for dinner?

Probably can his ass.

MARLEY DID ONE LAST SWEEP of the living room, making sure she'd dropped the clutter level from *this chick is a slob* to *organized mess*. She'd opted to serve Caleb dinner in the living room, since the kitchen reeked of paint. The Chinese food she'd ordered would be arriving any minute, and she'd already rid the coffee table of the paperback novels that usually resided there.

Now she stood in the doorway, wearing a pair of comfy black pants and her favorite stretchy green T-shirt. Butterflies danced around in her stomach.

"What am I doing?" she mumbled to herself, sinking down on the couch cushions.

She'd told Gwen she wasn't ready to get involved with anyone new, yet she seemed to be going out of her way to do just that. She pictured Caleb's face, wondering what it was about him that captivated her. Patrick had won her over with his easygoing smiles and almost youthful enthusiasm. He had a lust for life, charm that just poured out of him.

But Caleb...he was more intense. A little awkward around her, too, which she found kind of adorable. And whenever she thought about his hot kisses and lazy caresses, her body tightened with awareness.

Her head jerked up at the sound of the doorbell, immediately followed by the sound of her pulse drumming in her ears like the beat of a club song. She drew in a breath, willed her heartbeat to slow, then went to the door.

When she opened it, she found Caleb on the porch, wearing jeans and a long-sleeved navy-blue shirt, and holding two large paper bags with steam rolling out of the top. "I intercepted your delivery man at the door," he said.

Marley glanced past his impossibly broad shoulders, and saw the retreating headlights of a beat-up white Honda with Mr. Chow's logo on the side.

"I'll grab some cash and reimburse you," she said.

He shook his head. "No way."

"I said it would be my treat."

"I chose to ignore you." His deep voice brooked no argument as he entered her house.

"How very last century of you," she said sweetly.

He smiled—God, she loved it when he did that. "I'll take that as a compliment."

She led him into the living room, where they began laying out steaming hot cartons of food. Marley had already brought out plates and utensils, as well as a bottle of red wine and two glasses. She and Caleb got settled on the carpet, and she dug in immediately, too hungry to worry about the fact that she was stuffing her face when they'd barely said hello. She hadn't eaten a thing all day, thanks to another hectic shift at the hospital without a break and then because of the nervous flutters in her stomach at the prospect of seeing Caleb again.

She felt so drawn to the man, even though she still didn't know much about him, save for the fact that he was devastatingly handsome and kissed like a dream. Maybe tonight he'd finally open up to her a little.

"This is delicious," she moaned, popping another bite of sesame chicken into her mouth.

Caleb bit into an egg roll. "I haven't had Chinese food since I left New York. Back there, I live on this stuff."

"Is that where you call home?"

"I usually go where the job takes me," he answered.

She furrowed her brows. "You mean, for research?"

"No, I only started writing recently." He took another bite of the egg roll, then focused on the task of spooning chicken fried rice onto his plate. "I was doing construction before that, and the company I worked for did jobs all over the country."

"So you took time off to write?"

He nodded.

Marley picked up her wineglass, studying Caleb as she took a sip. He seemed completely uninterested in talking about himself. Patrick, on the other hand, had been all about his own ego, constantly regaling her with stories where he played the starring role. None of them true, of course.

Which did she prefer? A man who talked up a storm and only told lies? Or one who refused to talk at all? Still, she wasn't a quitter, and she was determined to pry some details out of Caleb.

"Does your family live on the East Coast?" she asked.

His face became shuttered. "I don't have any family. My mother died when I was five, and I never knew my dad."

She leaned closer, studied his face. "No aunts, uncles, grandparents?"

"Nope." His tone was casual, but she saw a flicker of pain in the depths of his eyes. He took a sip of wine, then said, "I was in foster care my whole childhood."

"Caleb, I—" Marley's words caught in her throat. "That must have been hard. What about close friends?"

Caleb's features creased with pain. "One. But he died a few months ago."

Her heart squeezed, just as it did in the hospital whenever she encountered a particularly sad case. "I'm sorry," she said quietly.

A lull fell over the room. Marley tried to focus on the food in front of her, but it was hard to ignore the flicker of sorrow on Caleb's face. She wondered how his friend had died, but didn't broach the subject. And he didn't share the details, making it obvious it wasn't a conversational path he wanted to venture down.

But his grief…she couldn't turn away from it. Couldn't ignore it, either. It was her fatal flaw. She saw someone in pain and felt compelled to help them. Setting down her fork, she slid closer to him, surprising them both when she lifted her hand to his face and traced the strong line of his jaw with her fingers.

"I'm sorry," she murmured again. "I know what it's like to lose someone close to you. When my mom died, it nearly tore my heart out."

Caleb covered her hand with his, but didn't move it away, just kept it pressed to his cheek. Slowly he turned his head to meet her gaze, and what she saw there stole the breath right out of her lungs. Heat. Lots and lots of heat, mixed in with that cloud of grief. His eyes dropped to her mouth.

He wanted to kiss her. His intentions were so clear they might as well be scrawled across a billboard in downtown San Diego. Yet he didn't make a single move. His cheek was hot beneath her palm, his hand just as warm as it covered her knuckles.

"Are you okay?" Her voice wavered.

A muscle in his jaw twitched. "No," he said roughly. "I never seem to be okay when you're around."

She didn't know what to make of the cryptic comment, and he didn't give her time to try and decipher it. He lowered his head and pressed his lips to hers.

Marley's entire body trembled. He tasted like soy sauce and wine and something distinctly male. And he kissed as if he actually gave a damn about kissing. Other men went through the motions, shoved their tongues into your mouth and made the appropriate groaning sounds, all the while wondering how they could move on to the more entertaining part of the evening.

Caleb, on the other hand, took his time. His lips and tongue toyed with her. He licked and nipped, as though he was sampling a mouthwatering dessert, a flavor he wanted to explore. Marley stroked his cheek, her hand tingling at the feel of his shadowy stubble chafing against her palm. Feeling bold, she slid her tongue into his mouth then retreated to sweep it across his bottom lip. She took the surprisingly soft flesh between her teeth and bit down gently, eliciting a low moan from deep in his throat.

He broke the kiss, tilting her head with one big hand so he could press his mouth to her neck. "You're a very dangerous woman," he rasped against her feverish skin.

She laughed. "Me? I'm the furthest thing from dangerous."

He left a trail of wet, open-mouthed kisses along her neck, his tongue traveling back to her lips, parting them and delving into her mouth again. This time, when he deepened the kiss, he brought his hands into play. They drifted down to her breasts, cupping the aching mounds through the fabric of her T-shirt, his thumbs flicking the nipples poking against her bra. Little sparks ignited in her belly, blazing a path up to her breasts, making them swell and tingle.

"No," he disagreed, pulling back so that his warm breath fanned across her lips. "You are dangerous."

With reluctance practically oozing from his pores, he dropped his hands from her chest and slid away from her, his broad back connecting with the edge of the sofa. "Which is why I need to focus on this delicious meal before I do something stupid." To punctuate the remark, he picked up his fork and speared it into the nearest carton, bringing out a tangle of spicy noodles.

"How about we skip dinner and go straight to dessert instead?"

The brazen suggestion flew out of her mouth before she could stop it. Once she'd said it, though, she knew she didn't want to take it back. Her breasts were heavy, achy. The tender spot between her legs quivered with need. Looking at Caleb, in the blue shirt that clung to his washboard abs, the dark hair falling on his forehead, the lust swimming in his eyes, she knew he was the only one who could soothe the ache.

The fork fell out of his hands and clattered onto his plate. He swallowed hard. "That's probably not a good idea."

"Why not?" She gave a wry smile. "Isn't sex always a good idea, according to guys?"

He coughed at the word *sex*. "Most believe that," he admitted. "But we've only just met, Marley."

He was right. She'd known him less than a week. But already she felt a connection to him. When he looked at her, she felt light-headed and vulnerable and so totally aroused. What would be so wrong about falling into bed with this man? She was old enough to know that sex didn't equal love and marriage. Sometimes it could just be about two people who were wildly attracted to each other, taking pleasure in what the other had to offer.

"Do you always date for at least six months before you sleep with someone?"

"No," he said. "But you're different."

"How so?"

"I don't know." His features furrowed with a hint of despair. "You just are."

She looked at him, and there it was again, that streak of white-hot chemistry, threatening to consume her whole. She wanted this. No, she *needed* it. Needed to feel wanted and appreciated. Needed to lose herself in this one passionate moment and forget about the stress and headaches of the last three months.

She rose to her feet. "Are you attracted to me?"

"You know I am." No hesitation on his part. She liked that. She also liked the way his eyes grew heavy-lidded, smoky with unconcealed desire.

"So let's do something about it."

Marley lowered her hands to the hem of her T-shirt. She brushed her fingers over the fabric, then lifted it just an inch, to reveal her midriff.

Caleb's breath hitched. "What are you doing?"

She raised her shirt another inch higher. "What do you think I'm doing?"

He gulped. "Marley..."

"For God's sake, Caleb, are you going to make me beg for it?"

Without waiting for an answer, she slid the shirt up her chest, over her head and threw it aside.

OH, LORD.

Caleb swallowed a few times, desperate to bring moisture to the arid desert his mouth had become. He couldn't tear his eyes off her. All that smooth, golden skin. The luscious, full breasts covered by a lacy white bra with a little pink bow. Christ, that bow. So proper and innocent and downright sexy. It drove him wild.

She drove him wild.

"Say something," she murmured.

He opened his mouth, but nothing came out. Every muscle in his body was taut, tight as a drum and wrought with tension that could only be eased by the thrust of his cock inside Marley Kincaid's sweet paradise. Oh, yeah, *paradise* was the word to describe her, all right. He could practically see her holding out the forbidden apple to him, her perfect skin and flat belly and out-of-this-world breasts taunting him to take a bite.

He stumbled to his feet and pressed his damp palms to his sides. Marley obviously took the action as a sign of assent because she moved closer, and closer, until they were mere inches apart. He knew he shouldn't be doing this. He was hunting her ex, for Pete's sake. So why couldn't he walk away?

His hand, of its own accord, touched her mouth, tracing the curve of her bottom lip. Her lips were red and swollen, the lips of a woman who'd just been thoroughly kissed.

Caleb smothered a wild curse. He'd been fantasizing about this woman for more than a week. He *craved* her.

But he couldn't have her. He gritted his teeth.

Her lips parted as she leaned into his touch. "Don't shut down on me," she said, as if reading his mind. "I know you want this, too."

He drew in a breath. Tried valiantly to resist the pure temptation she posed. Gathered up the courage to tell her he didn't want it, that it would be a mistake.

But then she touched him.

Just the feather-light brush of her fingers across his cheek and he was a goner. He kissed her, pouring all his frustration and pent-up lust into the kiss, pushing his tongue deep into her mouth until she was gasping with delight.

"Close the drapes," he choked out, pulling back.

She glanced at him in surprise. "What?"

"The drapes. They're wide open. Any of your neighbors could see us." One neighbor in particular. He wondered if AJ was watching. If he was shaking his head in disapproval.

"Shoot, you're right." She darted over to the window and shut the heavy drapes, officially closing out the world.

Closing out reality.

That's what he ought to be clinging to, reality, but it was too late now. The fantasy had taken over, and Caleb knew he could no longer walk away. He needed her too badly. Marley Kincaid had gotten under his skin from the second they'd met. He *had* to have her. He felt like an addict, and this insanely beautiful blonde was his fix. The only cure to the uncontrollable desire running rampant through his blood.

Marley sauntered back to him, her firm breasts swaying at each step. Lord, that bra scarcely covered her nipples. He could see the edge of her areolas. Dusky pink. Just as he'd imagined.

She stood inches away from him, her blond waves cascading down her bare shoulders. A moan lodged in the back of his throat. Before he could stop himself, he slid his fingers down her neck to caress her collarbone. Her skin was hot to the touch. Her sweet strawberry scent seized his senses and wrapped him in a hazy cloud of desire.

Marley stepped closer, pushed her barely covered breasts against him and whispered, "Your touch drives me crazy."

His pulse began to race. The fog in his brain deepened, making it impossible to form a coherent thought. His cock throbbed relentlessly, so stiff he could hardly move. He trailed his index finger up Marley's arm, stroking her shoulder, running his knuckles along the curve of her neck. She shivered.

"You have the softest skin I've ever felt," he murmured, then lowered his head to kiss the hollow at the base of her throat.

He looked up to see desire reflected in her deep-brown eyes, punctuated by her sharp intake of breath. "You're teasing me," she squeezed out.

He pressed his lips to her jaw, tongue darting out for a brief taste. "Do you want me to stop?" he asked in a rough voice.

"No."

Trying to ignore the heat flooding his groin, he moved his lips over hers. Softly, a mere hint of a kiss. She sighed into his mouth, rubbing her body against him like a contented little cat.

Capturing her bottom lip with his teeth, he swirled his tongue over it, then moved to lick her earlobe. He kissed the tender lobe, then her cheek, her jaw, her shoulder—everything but her lips, which were plump and moist and begging for attention.

She licked them, whispering, "Please," and finally he gave her what she wanted. What *he* wanted.

He claimed her mouth, and a rush of warmth assaulted him, pumping through his veins and making his pulse quicken. She tasted like heaven. As he possessed her lips, his hands cupped her mouthwatering breasts. He squeezed, then dipped his fingers under her lacy bra. Toyed with her nipples, pinched them, made them hard and stiff and watched as her eyelids closed and a moan of pleasure slid out of her throat.

"Please," she pleaded. "More."

Her hips moved restlessly, her pelvis sliding over the aching bulge in his pants. "More, Caleb, I need more."

He knew exactly what she meant. He needed more, too. So much more than he'd ever dreamed himself capable of wanting.

Swallowing, he reached between them and hooked his thumbs under the waistband of her pants. It was too late to stop this. Any of this. He was too far gone. And he knew that at this point, there was nothing he could do but hang on for the ride.

7

MARLEY'S ENTIRE BODY was on fire as Caleb peeled her pants off her legs and whipped them aside. That same fire smoldered in his blue eyes, the heat of it penetrating her bare skin. Something else flickered in his eyes, too. Wonder, maybe, and a hint of hesitation.

She reached out for him but he stepped back. "No," came his hoarse voice. "Just stand there for a second. Let me look at you."

Marley's arms dropped to her sides. Her cheeks warmed, but she didn't feel embarrassed. Caleb's gaze roamed every inch of her body, and each time he lingered, she grew hotter. Wetter. Nobody had ever looked at her like this before. As if she were the most beautiful thing in the world. And he was pretty damn beautiful at the moment, too. His eyelids were heavy, his handsome features creased with blatant sensuality. His breathing sounded labored. So was hers. In fact, if he didn't touch her soon, she feared she'd stop breathing altogether.

As if he'd read her mind, he moved closer and with

the softest of touches, grazed her collarbone with his thumb. "You're stunning," he murmured.

"You're exaggerating."

He shook his head, dead serious. "And you're underestimating yourself." He looked vaguely embarrassed. "I've fantasized about you since the day we met."

She swallowed. "Yeah?"

"Yeah." His fingers skimmed down her arm, then traveled toward her breasts, which tingled the second his strong hands came near.

He cupped her breasts and squeezed gently, eliciting a soft moan from her throat. Then he ran a finger under the edge of her bra and teased one rigid nipple. "Do you like this?" he asked quietly.

Pleasure coursed through her body, so strong she couldn't find her vocal cords. So she just nodded, her head lolling to the side as he continued teasing her.

Caleb reached for the front clasp of her bra and popped it open to expose her aching breasts. He sucked in his breath, the passion in his eyes darkening to midnight blue. "Tell me what you like, and what you don't." His voice was soft, his face slightly rueful. "I don't want to be too rough with you. I'm not always gentle."

He sounded genuine and awkward and she couldn't help but smile. God, who was this man? In her experience, men didn't usually take the time to find out what she liked. They just did what *they* liked.

She leaned her bare breasts into his waiting palms and said, "I like everything you do to me, Caleb."

A fleeting smile lifted the corner of his mouth, and then he lowered his head and pressed his lips to one throbbing breast, making her gasp. The heat of his mouth enclosed her nipple, his tongue darting out and swirling over the aching bud. And then he started to suck, so hard she nearly keeled over from the overwhelming wave of pleasure that crashed into her.

Caleb steadied her, rested one big hand on her hip while the other squeezed and fondled her chest. He shifted his head and tongued her other nipple. Sighed against her flesh as if he'd just discovered a treasure he hadn't believed existed. By the time the hand he'd placed on her hip slid to the juncture of her thighs, she was so wet and so hot and so ready she exploded almost immediately.

Marley cried out in a mixture of surprise and ecstasy as an orgasm that rivaled a category-5 hurricane slammed into her. Streaks of pleasure burned a trail through her body, growing more intense when Caleb rubbed his palm over her sex. She buried her face against his broad chest, shuddering violently, shamelessly writhing against his hand and taking every last iota of pleasure he could give her.

When she finally crashed back to earth, her pulse racing, her knees wobbling, she saw Caleb looking at her, his expression a combination of satisfaction and awe. Slowly, he slid her bikini panties down her legs, leaving her completely naked. And he was completely dressed.

"Gosh, you're such a tease. Are you going to take your clothes off sometime this century?" she grumbled, her core still throbbing from release.

Chuckling, Caleb reached for his collar, bunched the material between his fingers and yanked the shirt over his head. The sight of his bare chest sucked the remaining breath from her lungs. Smooth, tanned skin. Hard muscle and sleek sinew. A six-pack that made it extremely difficult not to drool…

"Better?" he taunted.

"Not yet." Her gaze followed the thin line of dark hair that arrowed down to the waistband of his jeans. "Take those off."

The corner of his mouth lifted. "If you insist."

Marley watched, mesmerized, as he tugged on the tab of his zipper. Her mouth went dry in anticipation. She couldn't wait to see him. All of him. Big and naked and—okay, so *big* was definitely the right word. Her thighs clenched at the sight of the long, thick erection revealed after he shucked his pants and boxers.

Caleb Ford was by far the sexiest man she had ever seen. His body was lean and solid, with muscular thighs, a trim waist and broad shoulders. She focused again on the impressive cock jutting toward her and before she could stop herself, she knelt down, bent forward and swiped her tongue along his tip.

Caleb jerked, a deep groan rumbling in his powerful chest. Emboldened, she took another taste, this time a long, slow lick along his shaft. He was velvety soft and rock-hard at the same time, and his salty, masculine taste made her sigh with pleasure.

"Who's the tease now?" he asked, one hand restlessly stroking her hair.

She looked up at him with a smile. "I'm not teasing. I'm exploring." Swirling her tongue over the pearly bead of moisture at his tip, she reached out and cupped his balls with one hand, squeezing gently.

This time his groan held a note of desperation. His grip on her hair tightened. He thrust his hips, his cock seeking her mouth. As little flames of excitement licked at her skin, she took him in her mouth and sucked.

"Yes," he hissed out. "That feels amazing."

His encouraging words sparked her confidence, inspiring her to take him in deeper. She purred against his hot shaft. She could feel him shaking, could feel the tension in his muscles, the raw passion building in his loins. His cock pulsed beneath her tongue. It thrilled her, knowing she was the one bringing him pleasure, the one stoking all that passion.

Caleb guided her head with his hand, groaning as she drew him in and out of her mouth, as she swirled her tongue over the tip of his cock at each upstroke.

She was just finding a rhythm, alternating between sharp pumps and long, lazy licks, when he made a strangled sound and withdrew. "I need to be in you, Marley."

He hauled her to her feet, nudging her so that she could sink down on the sofa. Then he faltered. "I didn't bring anything," he confessed.

"My purse," she squeezed out. "In the hall."

Nodding, he disappeared from the room, returning a moment later with her bag, which he handed to her instead of rifling through it himself. She found the plastic wrapper in the zippered pouch where she kept her mini first-aid kit. As a nurse, she was always prepared for everything.

Including, apparently, hot and impulsive living-room sex.

A hysterical laugh bubbled in the back of her throat as she hurriedly unwrapped the condom and handed it to Caleb.

He sheathed himself, looking at her with such longing and desire that she forgot how to breathe.

"Spread your legs wider for me," he whispered.

She obeyed him without question, as if spreading

her legs for this man was just another requirement for survival, like food, water, oxygen. Never breaking eye contact, Caleb stroked her tender folds with his thumb. He made a ragged sound in the back of his throat, his features taut with barely restrained lust.

Her thighs quivered. Parted even farther. Anticipation coiled inside her, but rather than sliding his thick erection where they both wanted it to be, he got to his knees first and pressed his mouth to her aching core.

When he captured her clit between his lips and suckled, she cried out, shocked to feel another spontaneous orgasm gathering in her belly. Ripples of pleasure danced along her skin, an unbearable fire of need building between her legs.

"I need you in me. Now." Her voice came out hoarse.

Before she could blink, his mouth left her, and his body covered hers. He positioned himself between her legs, then murmured, "Are you sure about this?"

She almost laughed. Her legs were wide open, his cock was prodding against her soaking-wet sex, and he was asking if she was sure? She wanted to say no, that she'd changed her mind, just to see what he'd do, but she had a feeling he would respect anything she said. Despite the fact that every muscle in his chest was straining with tension and his pulse throbbed in his neck, she knew he would stop if she asked, no matter how much pain he'd be in later.

Good thing she wasn't asking.

Gripping his strong chin with her hand, she pulled his mouth toward hers. "I'm more than sure," she said, and then she kissed him.

His tongue plunged into her mouth, and a second later, his erection followed suit and plunged inside her.

His thick cock filled her, stretching her in the most delicious way.

"You're so damn tight," he mumbled. "I'm afraid I'll hurt you."

Her heart did a little somersault. "I'll be fine."

She slid her hands down his back and found it covered by a sheen of sweat. The sinewy muscles there flexed beneath her fingers, tightening as he moved inside her with long, gentle strokes.

"You're holding back," she said, half teasing, half accusing.

His blue eyes flickered with uncertainty. "I'm too big for you. Are you sure you're okay?"

A laugh squeezed out of her throat. "Would you quit asking me if I'm sure about things? I'm dying here, Caleb."

His voice was husky as he said, "Me, too." Then he started to move. To *really* move. Marley let out a wild cry as he drove into her, his thrusts frantic. She curved her spine to take him in deeper, hooking her legs around his taut buttocks. The couch squeaked beneath them, cushions bouncing as Caleb pushed his cock in and out in a reckless pace that made her mind spin and her body throb.

Her breasts were crushed against him, nipples tingling as they brushed over the damp hairs on his chest. "You're amazing," he gasped, each word punctuated by the sharp thrusts of his hips.

She met his eyes, floored by the emotion she saw in them. He was looking at her as if she were the most beautiful creature on the planet, as if he couldn't possibly believe she was his for the taking.

Yanking his head down with her hands, she kissed him deeply, whimpering against his lips when he reached to where they joined and rubbed her clit with his thumb.

"Come with me, Marley."

He quickened his pace, filling her so deeply, so completely, it wasn't difficult to lose herself in another orgasm. As his fingers toyed with her clit, Marley arched her hips and toppled over the edge. Shards of light flashed before her, and her mind fragmented as a dizzying rush of pleasure flooded her body. Moaning, Caleb buried his face in the crook of her neck and shuddered as he gave himself over to a climax she suspected was as powerful as hers. His breath heated her neck, his cock twitching inside as he let go.

Their bodies were sticky with sweat, their breath coming out in ragged gasps. Marley wasn't sure which one of them started to laugh first, but they were both chuckling when Caleb finally lifted himself up on his elbows and brushed his lips over hers in a tender kiss.

"Wow," she said with another laugh. "That was... wow."

Amusement joined the remnants of release in his eyes. "Yeah," he laughed. "You're right."

Looking reluctant, he slid out of her, his gaze roaming over her naked body. She noticed a rosy blush dotting her breasts and moisture still pooled between her legs. She was amazed to realize she could go again. All he needed to do was shove that wicked cock back inside her and she'd be ready for him.

As if reading her thoughts, Caleb's shoulders squared in determination, and then he gripped her waist and hoisted her up to her feet. She squeaked in surprise. "What are you doing?"

"Carrying you upstairs." True to his words, he cupped her ass with one hand and lifted her into his powerful arms, holding her there as though she weighed no more than a feather. "Come on, we need a bed."

WHILE HIS HEART THUDDED against his ribs like a pair of fists, Caleb rolled off Marley's body and sucked in a gulpful of air. His cock twitched against his belly, throbbing from its third release of the night. He was still as hard as a slab of marble, and when he glanced at Marley, the haze of desire in her brown eyes told him she was nowhere near sated, either.

Hands down, he'd just had the best sex of his life. Three times. He couldn't think of any past encounter that even compared to what he'd experienced with Marley. The sheer thrill of sliding into her tight core. The body-numbing releases. He almost felt cheated. He'd always enjoyed sex, but this...this was sex to the max.

"Do you want to spend the night?" Marley murmured. "I don't have to get up early tomorrow." She moved closer and nestled her head in the crook of his neck.

Caleb ran his fingers through her sweat-dampened hair and stared up at the ceiling. The bedroom was dark—his doing, of course. He knew how transparent those damn curtains of hers were, and the last thing he wanted was AJ catching any glimpses of what he and Marley were doing.

The thought of AJ brought a rush of guilt so strong he nearly choked on it. Lord, what was he doing? The implications of what he'd done settled over him like a thick cloud of smog. He'd lied to her. He'd spied on her. Videotaped her.

Slept with her.

He'd always considered himself a man of honor, a man with principles, but he'd thrown honor right out the window when he'd succumbed to temptation.

He had to give her the truth. Shards of pain pierced his stomach at the thought. She trusted him, damn it. He saw that trust glimmering in her eyes like diamonds. How could he possibly tell her she'd been duped—*again?*

The confession burned in his chest, but he couldn't reveal the truth now. She'd kick him out, and then who would be there to protect her if Grier showed up?

"Caleb?" Her voice cut through his thoughts. "Are you staying?"

He swallowed. "Yeah, I'll stay."

"Good, because I'm way too tired to walk you out."

With a contented little sigh, she pulled the bedspread up and over the two of them. Then she slung one slender arm over his bare chest and gave another purr of pleasure.

"You realize you wore me out, right? I'm lucky I don't have to work tomorrow or I'd probably doze off in the middle of removing a catheter," she said with a sleepy laugh.

He continued stroking her hair, then stopped abruptly when he realized the gesture felt too damn right.

Okay, it was official. He was in deep, deep trouble here. Sleeping with Marley was one thing, but cuddling? Petting her? Whispering in the darkness? This was not good. In fact, all this non-sex stuff was far more dangerous than sex itself. It was relationship stuff. Commitment stuff. And he definitely didn't do either of those.

He had tried making connections over the years.

He'd latched on to his first few foster mothers, pathetically begging for their love, only to be carted off to another house within months. After that, he got smart. What was the point in opening yourself up to another person when they would only kick you aside sooner or later?

Smothering a sigh, he forced the memories from his head. "Did you always want to be a nurse?" he found himself asking.

She was silent for a moment. "No."

Her response aroused his curiosity. "What did you want to be then?"

He gave an inward groan after he'd spoken. What was wrong with him? Why was he so fascinated by her? He couldn't for the life of him remember ever asking the woman in his bed what she wanted to be when she grew up. He didn't care about things like that. Didn't care about anything but getting pleasure and giving it right back.

Until now. Now, he couldn't seem to stop himself from wanting to know everything about this woman.

"I was accepted to the fine arts program at UCLA," she confessed. "I've always loved art. Creating things."

"I can tell," he said, thinking about how passionately she'd thrown herself into making her house look beautiful. "So what happened?"

"My mom was admitted to the hospital." Marley's voice shook. "She was in so much pain. The cancer… it destroyed her inside and out, and I would sit by her side watching it, wishing I could do something to help her."

She fell silent again. Caleb waited for her to continue, all the while trying to ignore the strange somersaults his heart was doing.

"I enrolled in nursing school the day after she died," Marley finally said. "I couldn't help my mom, but that way I could at least help other people."

It suddenly became extremely hard to breathe. She had become a nurse because she hadn't been able to help her mother in her dying hours. God, what a woman. Shame gripped his gut in a tight vise. And here he was, lying to her.

"How did your mom die?" Marley asked, her tone gentle.

"Overdose." He'd been prepared to avoid the question, maybe even pretend to be asleep, so when that one word burst out of his mouth, he was overcome with shock. Why had he just told her that?

"And you were five?" she pressed, obviously remembering the meager details he'd provided.

"Yeah." It became difficult to draw a breath. "I was watching TV in our bedroom—we only had one bedroom in the apartment—and I went out to the living room to ask about dinner and…she was just lying there on the carpet." His chest went impossibly tight. "I remember shaking her, crying for her to wake up, but… she didn't wake up. She was already dead."

"Oh, Caleb," Marley whispered. "That's awful. I'm so sorry you had to go through that."

He tried to shrug it off. "I got over it."

There was a short silence, and then Marley released a small sigh. "I'm so sorry," she said again, turning her head to press a tender kiss to his chest.

What was the matter with him? Why had he told her about his mother? He hadn't even told Russ about that day, and Russ had been his best friend. His only friend.

He lay very still, trying to navigate the confusion

clouding his brain. This wasn't supposed to happen. He wasn't supposed to sleep with her. To share his past with her.

Growing up, he'd been guided by a sense of justice, going into drug enforcement because it was the only way he knew to find some sort of vengeance for his mother's death. He lived his life by a code of honor. There was a distinct line between right and wrong.

But Marley was blurring that line. His body ached at the feel of Marley snuggled up close to him. He listened to her breathing grow steady, felt her muscles loosen with slumber, and as he lay there beside her, he realized she was far more dangerous than he'd given her credit for.

8

MARLEY WOKE UP the next morning with a smile on her face and a naked man in her bed. Caleb was sound asleep beside her, lying on his stomach with one strong arm flung over her belly. Her smile widened. God, he was breathtaking. His stubble-covered cheek rested against the pillow, his dark hair messy and falling onto his proud forehead. And his face lost all of its hard edges in slumber. He looked peaceful, younger.

Trying not to wake him, she moved his arm and slid out of bed. Then she walked into the washroom, heading for the small shower stall. A jolt of pain hit her big toe.

"Shoot," she muttered, noticing that one of the tiles was loose. Good thing she was planning on retiling after she finished painting.

She opened the glass door of the shower stall, and as she turned the faucet and adjusted the temperature, she realized she was actually pretty sore. A slight ache between her legs, but one she was willing to overlook because last night had been totally worth it. She stepped into the shower and dunked her head under

Send For
2 FREE BOOKS
Today!

I accept your offer!

Please send me two
free Harlequin® Blaze®
novels and two mystery
gifts (gifts worth about $10).
I understand that these books
are completely free—even the
shipping and handling will be
paid—and I am under no obligation
to purchase anything, ever, as explained
on the back of this card.

151/351 HDL FEHC

Please Print

FIRST NAME

LAST NAME

ADDRESS

APT.#   CITY

STATE/PROV.   ZIP/POSTAL CODE

Visit us online at
www.ReaderService.com

Offer limited to one per household and not applicable to series that subscriber is currently receiving.

Your Privacy—The Reader Service is committed to protecting your privacy. Our Privacy Policy is available online at www.ReaderService.com or upon request from the Reader Service. We make a portion of our mailing list available to reputable third parties that offer products we believe may interest you. If you prefer that we not exchange your name with third parties, or if you wish to clarify or modify your communication preferences, please visit us at www.ReaderService.com/consumerchoice or write to us at Reader Service Preference Service, P.O. Box 9062, Buffalo, NY 14269. Include your complete name and address.

The Reader Service—Here's how it works: Accepting your 2 free books and 2 free gifts (gifts valued at approximately $10.00) places you under no obligation to buy anything. You may keep the books and gifts and return the shipping statement marked "cancel". If you do not cancel, about a month later we'll send you 6 additional books and bill you just $4.49 each in the U.S. or $4.96 each in Canada. That is a savings of at least 14% off the cover price. It's quite a bargain! Shipping and handling is just 50¢ per book in the U.S. and 75¢ per book in Canada.* You may cancel at any time, but if you choose to continue, every month we'll send you 6 more books, which you may either purchase at the discount price or return to us and cancel your subscription.

*Terms and prices subject to change without notice. Prices do not include applicable taxes. Sales tax applicable in N.Y. Canadian residents will be charged applicable taxes. Offer not valid in Quebec. Credit or debit balances in a customer's account(s) may be offset by any other outstanding balance owed by or to the customer. Please allow 4 to 6 weeks for delivery. Offer available while quantities last. All orders subject to credit approval. Books received may not be as shown.

▼ If offer card is missing write to: The Reader Service, P.O. Box 1867, Buffalo, NY 14240-1867 or visit www.ReaderService.com ▼

NO POSTAGE
NECESSARY
IF MAILED
IN THE
UNITED STATES

BUSINESS REPLY MAIL
FIRST-CLASS MAIL   PERMIT NO. 717   BUFFALO, NY

POSTAGE WILL BE PAID BY ADDRESSEE

THE READER SERVICE
PO BOX 1867
BUFFALO NY 14240-9952

the hot spray, then turned to let the water slide down her body.

Her muscles sighed with relief as the water pounded against them. She was on her feet nearly every day of the week and did yoga regularly, but one night with the talented Caleb Ford had completely wiped her out. It had never been like that with anyone, not even Patrick.

The smile on her face faded as the memory of the last man she'd been with pushed its way into her head and the implication of what she'd done settled over her. Was she crazy? After what had happened with Patrick, she'd vowed to be more cautious, and yet she'd just slept with a man she'd known for less than a week.

She slowly lathered her skin with strawberry-scented body wash, forcing her mind to quit overanalyzing. It was just sex. Really great sex. Wasn't like she'd gotten engaged to the man.

Shutting off the faucet, she toweled off and left the bathroom, slipped into a pair of denim shorts and a red tank, and turned her attention to the man on the bed.

He was wide awake, and sporting a very familiar expression on his face.

The same shuttered stare he'd donned yesterday when he'd told her sleeping together wasn't a good idea.

"I'm going to make some breakfast," she announced. "Do you like pancakes?"

"I love them," he said quietly.

"Good. They'll be ready by the time you come down."

She headed downstairs, trying to forget about how stiff his shoulders had looked. Maybe he simply wasn't a morning person. Like her brother—Sam could be a total ass before he had his morning coffee.

When Caleb walked into the kitchen ten minutes

later, his hair damp from the shower and his blue eyes alert, she handed him a cup of freshly brewed coffee.

"Thanks." He took it gratefully, and sipped the hot liquid.

Marley moved back to the stove and flipped a pancake, wishing he wasn't being so distant. It was easy to pick up on the waves of tension rolling off him. Finally she turned to him and asked, "Everything okay?"

He didn't speak for a moment, just headed to the kitchen table and lowered his big body onto a chair. A line of indecision creased his forehead, and when he opened his mouth, she got the feeling she wouldn't like what he said.

"I'm fine. Just tired," he said with a shrug.

"Well, hopefully these will help." She turned off the burner, then walked over to the table and placed a plate loaded with pancakes in front of him.

Almost instantly, his expression perked up. She suppressed a grin. Men and their stomachs.

He inhaled the delicious aroma of blueberries and buttermilk, and groaned. "You neglected to mention you could cook like this."

"I only do breakfast," she clarified as she sat across the table. "For some reason it's all I can manage. Lunch and dinner? I'm lucky I haven't burned down the kitchen yet."

Caleb chuckled. "Thank God for that."

She picked up her knife and fork and cut her pancake in half, then fourths, then eighths. She noticed Caleb watching her in amusement as she finally brought a bite-size piece to her lips.

"You cut it up in advance?" he said with a laugh.

She finished chewing and shot him an indignant

look. "It's all ready to eat that way. No wasting time after each bite."

"You could always cut the next piece while you chew," he pointed out.

"Don't be a smart ass. Eat your breakfast."

She was pleased to see him devour the pancakes. For some reason, she liked making him happy. She got the feeling Caleb wasn't the kind of man who'd been served fluffy pancakes very often. There was an edge to him, something raw and vulnerable at times.

This morning, that edge seemed sharper than ever. He didn't say much as he drank his coffee. His dark eyebrows were furrowed, and he looked as if some inner dilemma was tearing him up.

"You okay?" Marley asked again, as she poured a hefty amount of syrup on her second pancake.

"Yeah. I'm fine." Setting down his cup, Caleb stood. He grabbed his dish and headed for the sink, keeping his back to her as he rinsed his plate under the faucet.

"You don't have to do that," Marley called. "I'll just shove everything into the dishwasher later."

"I can't not do the dishes after I eat," he replied without turning around. "It's a habit I picked up when I lived in one of my foster homes. My foster mom used to give me a quarter every time I cleaned up after myself."

"That was sweet of her," Marley remarked.

"Yeah, I guess it was. She was one of the nicer ones." She heard the smile in his voice. "She gave me this cracked yellow piggy bank to put the quarters into. I kept every quarter. I thought if I saved them all, I would have enough money to run away and be on my own." His shoulders tensed. "Not that it mattered. One of my foster brothers stole every last penny the night before he was transferred to another home."

Her heart melted in her chest, sympathy for that lost little boy tightening her stomach. "Caleb...I'm sorry."

She pushed away her plate and got up, walking over to him with purposeful strides. His back stiffened at her approach. She knew he probably felt uncomfortable for revealing what was obviously a painful memory. He'd looked and sounded the same way last night, when he'd told her about his mother's death.

"Sorry, didn't mean to depress you," he remarked.

She rested her hand on his arm and stroked the curve of his bicep. "It's okay to talk about things that hurt you," she said. "I do it all the time."

"I'm not great with talking about my feelings, or my past." His voice sounded thick as he admitted what she already knew.

Still, it might have been one of the most honest sentences he'd ever spoken to her, and she rose up on her tiptoes and kissed him, a slow, deep kiss filled with gratitude and warmth. He responded instantly, slipping his tongue between her parted lips and exploring her mouth with what felt almost like desperation.

Her heartbeat quickened. She wondered if every kiss she shared with Caleb would be like this. The racing pulse, the damp palms, the melting of her body into his. He placed his hand on the back of her head and drew her closer, teasing her with his mouth, his lips, his tongue. The air in the kitchen felt charged, like the streak of arousal crackling through her blood.

"Marley?"

She and Caleb broke apart like a pair of teenagers caught necking in a parked car. She swiveled her head and saw her brother in the doorway.

"What the hell is going on here?" Sam asked, his gaze shifting from her to Caleb. "Who is *he?*"

Marley found her voice. "*He* is Caleb. My, um, neighbor."

Her brother strode to the middle of the room and eyed Caleb like a guard dog that had just discovered a burglar in the house. Too bad Sam was more like a cocker spaniel than a rottweiler. In his sky-blue surf shorts and white T-shirt, with his blond hair windswept as usual, her brother posed the least menacing picture Marley could conjure up.

"Do you always make out with your neighbors?" Sam demanded.

"Just the cute ones," she replied.

Caleb snorted, then stuck out his hand. "I take it you're Marley's brother. It's nice to meet you."

Sam looked at Caleb's outstretched hand warily, but the good manners their parents had instilled in them beat out his obvious desire to play the role of Angry Brother. He shook Caleb's hand and said, "I'm Sam." His eyes narrowed. "Why are you kissing my sister?"

Caleb looked so uncomfortable she took pity on him and said, "Because we're seeing each other."

Sam's dark-blond eyebrows shot to his forehead. He glanced over at Marley. "Since when?"

"This week," she admitted.

"And you didn't tell me?"

"I don't tell you everything." Before Sam could continue the cross-examination, she said, "What are you doing here, anyway? Finally going to finish the hall closet?"

"Tomorrow. Dad's barbecuing for lunch," Sam said with a sigh. "He wants you to come."

"He sent you all the way over here to invite me to lunch? You could have just called, you know."

Sam shrugged. "I had to take measurements of the closet. I'm picking up some supplies before I come over tomorrow." He shot her a pointed look. "I'm glad I came, otherwise I would have never known about your new *boyfriend*."

Marley's cheeks heated up. "When's the barbecue?"

"In a couple of hours, but Dad wants you to come earlier. He has something to show you."

Marley blanched. "Oh, God. Is it what I think it is?"

For the first time since he'd marched inside, Sam broke out a lopsided grin. "Sure is."

Caleb shot her a quizzical look. "Do I get to be in the loop?"

She laughed. "Nope. Trust me, you have to see it to believe it." To Sam, she said, "Can you call Dad and tell him to expect a guest?"

The suspicion on her brother's face returned. "Sure, I guess." Shoulders stiff, he turned for the door. "I'll just take those measurements and meet you over at the house."

After Sam left the kitchen, Marley gave Caleb an apologetic glance. "Sorry, I didn't even think to ask you if you wanted to come along. I can tell them you can't make it."

He hesitated for a long time, but then to her surprise, asked, "Would you like me to go?"

She pondered the question. Would she? It might be awkward for him. Since Patrick's arrest and escape, the men in Marley's life had become super-protective. Sam, despite the fact that he was younger, now acted as if his only goal in life was to monitor and ensure her well-being, and their father wasn't much better. Each time she saw him, her dad quizzed her about every aspect of her life.

She wasn't sure how he would react when he met Caleb. Neither he nor Sam had liked Patrick, which only made her feel like a bigger fool. What had they seen that she hadn't?

But Caleb was different. He wasn't as smooth and polished as Patrick. Definitely not as talkative, either. And who knew, maybe her family would see something in him that she wasn't picking up on. She still didn't fully trust her instincts. It might not be a bad thing to gauge her family's reaction to Caleb.

"I'd like it if you came," she finally said.

He nodded. "All right then."

She leaned up and planted a kiss against his cheek. "Thank you."

THIRTY MINUTES AFTER they arrived at Marley's childhood home, Caleb was regretting his decision to join her. He should have stayed back at the Strathorn house. But he hadn't wanted to leave her side, especially with the chance that Grier was keeping tabs on her. Away from the safety of her home, Marley made an easy target, and Caleb refused to let her out of his sight.

But he knew he was totally out of his element here. He was a trained government agent. He'd arrested, interrogated and physically struggled with the slime of the world. Yet he was intimidated by a twenty-four-year-old guy in surf shorts and a salt-and-pepper-haired father in the process of showing off a castle he'd built.

Out of Popsicle sticks.

"It's…interesting," Caleb remarked as he stared, stupefied, at the structure.

The castle was about two feet wide and three feet

tall, made up of hundreds—no, had to be in the thousands—of little wooden sticks. Some were intact, creating walls and turrets. Others had been cut to accommodate little windows and doors. Oh, and a drawbridge. Who could overlook the drawbridge?

Next to him, Marley seemed to be fighting a grin. "Dad's very passionate about his hobby."

Sam Sr. lovingly picked up his creation from the crate it had been sitting on and set it on one of the long work tables in the garage. His brown eyes, the same shade as his daughter's, were animated. "My best one yet, don't you think, honey?"

"Definitely," she agreed.

Marley's dad linked his arm through hers and led her out of the garage. Caleb trailed after them as they stepped onto the driveway. He kept a watchful eye on their surroundings, determined to stay on guard during this visit.

His gaze focused on the intertwined arms of Marley and her father, and he was unable to stop the envy that rolled around in his chest. He could tell just by looking at them that they were close. And the way Sam Sr.'s eyes filled with warmth each time he looked at his daughter was almost painful to watch. Caleb had never had anything even close to that growing up. He'd known families like this existed, but he hadn't seen it up close before.

They walked around the side of the sprawling, Spanish-style bungalow and stepped into the spacious backyard. The grass was perfectly mowed, colorful flowers popped up around the perimeter, and the array of birdhouses and feeders hanging from the trees made Caleb smile. Evidently one of her father's hobbies had rubbed off on Marley.

Sam was manning the barbecue, flipping burgers with a spatula. He glanced up at their approach and grinned at his sister. "It's your turn to set the table, kiddo."

Marley let go of her dad's arm and took a step toward the patio door. "I'll help you," Caleb offered.

"No, sit down, relax," she called over her shoulder.

As Marley darted into the house, Caleb awkwardly crossed the stone patio and sank into one of the chairs by the large table. Marley's dad joined him. The older man settled into his chair, then fixed a frown in Caleb's direction. "So. Marley mentioned you're a writer?"

"Yes, sir." He swallowed, wondering why the lie that had come so easily a week ago now stuck in his throat.

"My wife was a writer," the older man revealed.

"Really? What did she write?"

"Articles, mainly. She freelanced for some of the top home and garden magazines in the country." Marley's father swept his arm in the direction of the garden. "This garden was her showpiece."

"There was even a feature about it in *Good House-keeping*," Marley chimed in, coming outside in time to hear her father's remark. She set four plates on the table, along with drinking glasses, utensils and a tray of condiments, then flopped down in the chair next to Caleb's.

"The garden is really pretty," Caleb remarked. "Who maintains it?"

"I do," Sam Sr. answered with a proud smile. "Before Jessie passed, I promised her I would do right by her babies." He winked. "The kids *and* the flowers."

"Well, you're doing a good job," Caleb said, and meant it.

"Food's ready," Sam boomed from across the patio. A moment later, he strode across the pink and gray stones and dropped a platter of burgers on the table.

Despite the fact that he'd eaten breakfast only two hours earlier, Caleb's mouth watered at the aroma of ground beef and melted cheese. Marley's brother joined them at the table, and the four of them didn't say much as they fixed their burgers and settled back to eat.

Caleb's eyes met Marley's. He found himself fighting a grin when he noticed a splotch of ketchup at the corner of her mouth.

Her brother noticed, too, and guffawed. "We eat food here, not wear it."

Shooting her brother a dirty look, Marley reached for a napkin and wiped demurely at her mouth. "Can it, Sammy."

"Would you like me to get you a bib?" he returned with a smirk.

Caleb choked down a laugh. At the same time, he wanted to hightail it out of here. This was too damn surreal. The bickering siblings. The father looking on in gentle amusement. The homemade burger patties and bright-pink petunias and napkins with little dancing goats on them.

This wasn't his life. This wasn't *anyone's* life, was it? Lord, it was bad enough that he'd slept with Marley under false pretenses, but hanging out with her family? A wave of discomfort crested in his stomach, especially when Marley offered a snarky comment to her brother, and Sam Sr. grinned at Caleb. Crap. Marley's dad was warming up to him. Heck, so was her brother. After an initial bout of curt sentences and suspicious looks, the two men were now beginning to drop their guard.

As lunch progressed, Sam Sr. spoke to Caleb about the east coast, where he'd apparently lived for a few years following college. And the younger Sam spoke at length about their construction business. From the sound of it, the business wasn't booming, but it paid the mortgage, and both Kincaid men obviously enjoyed the work.

They perked up when Caleb mentioned he'd worked construction in the past, and he found himself enjoying talking to them about it. His fake writing career was a topic he avoided, but since construction was something he'd actually done before the DEA, he felt comfortable discussing it, and Marley's family seemed to warm up to him even more.

By the time the food was gone and the table was cleared, Caleb's chest felt as if it were being squeezed in a vise. These people were...*nice*. They cared about each other. They *respected* each other. It was so unlike most of the families he'd been around growing up. The abusive foster fathers, the alcoholic mothers, the dilapidated houses, soiled sheets and empty refrigerators.

"You okay?" Marley murmured, flashing a tentative smile in his direction.

Next to her, Sam Sr. and his son were still talking about the renovation job they were currently working on.

Caleb lowered his voice. "I'm fine. I just spaced out for a second." Fortunately, his cell began to vibrate in his pocket before she could press him. "Excuse me for a second," he said, barely able to hide his relief as he pulled out the phone.

He left the table and walked a few feet away,

standing near the barbecue as he checked his phone. Nobody was calling, but a series of text messages were coming through, all from AJ.

Tech guys at SDPD tracked the email to an IP addy downtown. Beachside Internet Café. Grier used free email account, registered with fake name.

The next message beeped in.

Staff couldn't ID Grier from pic. Barista remembers guy in baseball cap, sunglasses, looked shady, but she didn't see his face.

A final text popped up.

Give me a couple of hours before you bring her home. Wiring got screwed up. Two monitors are down. Gotta fix them.

He put away the cell, experiencing only a fleeting spark of disappointment. He'd known Grier's message would be a dead end. The man was too smart to send an email from his personal account, or to register for a new one under his real name.

Caleb glanced at Marley. She was amused by something her brother had said, her blond hair bouncing over her slender shoulders as her body vibrated with laughter. She looked unbelievably beautiful in her old denim shorts and thin red tank top. Her face was shining, her plump lips curved with delight as another burst of laughter rolled out of her chest.

He suddenly pictured how she'd look when she

found out the truth about who he was. The shine in her eyes would fade to a dull matte. Those lips would tighten with fury. Her joy would fizzle like a candle in the rain.

Caleb bent his head and pretended to text something on his phone, his blood pressure rising. He'd screwed up, given in to temptation and now he had to live with the knowledge that he'd deceived a woman he was really starting to care about.

Marley would never forgive him for lying to her.

He was also pretty certain that he'd never be able to forgive himself.

GODDAMN ADULTEROUS *BITCH*.

Patrick could barely contain the streaks of fury shooting through his body like hot bolts of lightning. He'd been standing by the window for the past hour, still stunned by what he'd seen. The cop, strolling out of Marley's house at ten o'clock in the morning. And then the two of them getting into the cop's shiny Range Rover an hour later, going off to who knew where.

Patrick had watched Mr. DEA arrive on Marley's porch the evening before, and all night he'd paced the bedroom, his anger building, growing, until his gut was knotted with wrath.

That whore.

She'd slept with the cop. At the start of the evening, Patrick had tried making excuses for her. She was just being nice. A friendly neighbor. But he was all out of excuses.

Marley had slept with another man.

His Marley had let another man touch her.

Patrick drew his arm back and sent it smashing into the wall.

A frightened gasp sounded from the bed, where Lydia White lay in fear.

He ignored her, didn't even feel the pain in his hand. Nor did he pay much attention to the neat hole he'd just punched in Lydia's drywall. The acidic taste of betrayal burned in his mouth, making him want to unleash another upper cut at something else. Mainly the jerk who'd just had sex with his girlfriend.

Releasing a strangled shout, Patrick edged toward the canopy bed and sank down on the ugly flowered bedspread. His heart thudded, each sharp beat vibrating with rage and desperation.

"How could she do this to me?" he demanded, staring at Lydia. "Everything I've done the past few months was for her. Do you think I like hiding out in this shit hole, staring at your wrinkled old face? I could have left the country months ago!"

But he hadn't. He'd been getting cash together, calling his contacts in South America to help him disappear, arranging for new identities for him and Marley.

And instead of being patient, instead of trusting that he would take care of her, she'd gone out and slept with the first guy to come knocking at her door. Ungrateful little bitch.

Patrick dropped his head in his hands. Rubbed his aching temples.

"I can't let her get away with this," he mumbled.

Lydia let out a muffled yelp, beginning to struggle against the duct tape binding her hands and legs.

"Shut up," he snapped. "Just. Shut. Up."

How could Marley betray him? How *could* she?

Patrick slowly uncurled his fists and took a long,

calming breath. Fine, so she'd screwed around on him. Big deal. He'd get over it.

But first…

First he had to make Marley pay for what she'd done to him.

9

"THIS WAS A GOOD IDEA," Marley said, shooting Caleb a smile that made the drive to Coronado worth the traffic they'd encountered on the way.

Caleb watched as she dug her bare toes into the soft warm sand of Coronado Beach. After leaving the Kincaid house, he'd suggested coming to the beach in order to give AJ enough time to take care of the security cameras. His partner had said a couple of hours, but Caleb didn't want to risk bringing Marley back too early. He'd raised the beach idea on impulse, but now that they were here, he was glad they'd come. The tranquil turquoise water lapping against the shore a few yards away soothed him, making him feel more relaxed than he had in months.

Still, he remained vigilant, just in case Grier had followed them.

"I can't imagine growing up here," he admitted, looking out at the water. "It's so different from the east coast."

"Yeah, I don't think I'd like it over there," Marley said. "I would miss the Pacific Ocean too much."

"The Atlantic isn't bad," he protested. "Just a little cold."

She snorted. "A *little* cold? Tell that to the passengers of the *Titanic*."

She slid a hair elastic off her wrist and tied her hair up in a messy twist. Wavy strands framed her face and Caleb reached out to tuck some behind her ears. She smiled, then took his hand, interlacing her fingers with his.

"Thanks for coming to my dad's today," she told him as they moved closer to the water.

They'd taken off their shoes and left them on the sand, and the warm water splashed over Caleb's toes. The late-afternoon breeze felt like a soft caress on his face, the scent of sand and salt bringing a wave of serenity over him. Yet, even as his muscles loosened and his face tipped up to soak in the sun, in the back of his mind he couldn't stop thinking about how Marley would react when he told her who he really was.

On the drive out here, he'd considered not telling her at all. Just packing up and taking off, letting another agent handle the stakeout and the hunt for Grier. He knew Marley would be hurt, sure, but better a minor broken heart than another major dose of betrayal. But now, as he watched her smiling at a squawking seagull that swooped by, as the warmth of her fingers seeped into his palm, he knew he couldn't leave without telling her the truth. After all the lies Grier had told her, she deserved honesty.

"My dad likes you," she said. "Sam does, too, but he probably won't admit it."

"He's just being protective. I'm sure they were both pretty shocked and pissed off when they found out about Patrick."

Marley dropped her eyes. "Yeah, they were. But I don't think anyone was as shocked as I was."

Caleb tightened his grip on her hand. "You shouldn't blame yourself. It sounds like your ex was a pretty smooth liar."

"Let's not talk about him anymore," Marley said suddenly. "It's such a beautiful day. I don't want to spoil it."

"What do you want to talk about then?"

"I don't know. Anything. Tell me something. What do you do in New York when you're not working?"

Caleb scrubbed his free hand through his hair. "Honestly? Not much, really."

It was true. Now that he thought about it, he rarely took time off. It was one assignment after the next, and when he did have some down time, he usually spent it consulting with other agents about *their* cases. He and Russ had played poker every now and then, gone out to a bar a few times, but his partner had been a workaholic, too.

"You don't go out? Ball games? Movies?" Marley prompted.

"Nope. I just work."

She sighed. "There's more to life than work, you know."

"Not for me."

"Do you ever get attached to people, or are you only attached to your job?"

A wave of discomfort swelled inside him. He'd heard this before, from women he'd had casual flings with, women looking to turn it into something more. Somehow, though, hearing the criticism come from Marley bugged him. So what if the only real relationship he had was with his job? Was it really that unusual?

"My job is all I need," he said with a shrug.

Marley shot him a knowing glance. "That's what I thought, too, ever since Patrick took off. I told myself I didn't need anything or anybody else."

"And now you need that?"

"Need, no. But I want it." A smile stretched across her face. "It's because of you, you know."

His mouth ran dry. "Yeah?"

"I'm having fun again, Caleb, thanks to you. You reminded me that there are still some good guys left in the world."

Self-reproach crushed his chest. "Marley," he started, his voice thick. "I wanted to tell you—"

She cut him off with a kiss. He tried to pull back, but the feel of her lips on his drained all common sense from his brain. As Marley looped her arms around his neck, he curled his fingers over her slender hips and bent down to deepen the kiss. Their tongues danced. His pulse sped up.

"How do you always manage to do that to me?" she said breathlessly.

"Do what?"

"Turn me on so hard, so fast." She laughed. "You have a gift."

Caleb took her hand and guided it to the bulge in his jeans. "I think you're the one with the gift," he sighed.

He nearly came apart as she gently rubbed his erection. With a strangled groan, he moved her hand and said, "We're not alone."

Marley looked around, her eyes widening when she spotted another couple walking hand-in-hand on the beach, as well as three teenagers horsing around in the water a hundred yards away.

She laughed again. "Okay, I guess you can add

making me forget my surroundings to the list of things you're good at." Her brown eyes sparkled. "Wanna get out of here?"

Hesitation crept up his spine. He knew exactly what they would do if they left the beach and went back to her place, and talking wouldn't be on the agenda. If they stayed here, out in public, he could fight the temptation to tear her clothes off and muster up enough courage to tell her the truth.

But then Marley kissed him again, and the wave of lust that hit him was so powerful he could barely remember his own name, let alone anything else.

She took his hand and led him toward the narrow staircase leading up to the parking lot where they'd left his car. He followed her blindly, unable to combat the potent force of desire pulling him. When they reached the car, Marley hopped in, her enthusiasm bringing a smile to his lips.

He shut the driver's door and moved to start the engine, but Marley intercepted his hand. Before he could blink, she climbed onto his lap.

Heat coiled in his belly at the feel of her firm thighs straddling him. "What are you doing?" he choked out.

"What do you think?"

His cock thickened as she unbuttoned her shorts and began to wiggle out of them. All the wiggling succeeded in making him even harder. Fire seared through his blood, his mind turning to mush. All he could do was lean back and let her take control. Tossing her shorts onto the passenger seat, she stroked him over the denim then unzipped his jeans.

A streak of raw lust shot through him. He'd never done it in front of audience, but the notion of getting caught was an odd turn-on. There were no other cars in the lot, but someone could pull in at any moment.

Marley must have considered it, too, because as she slowly drew him out of his pants, she glanced out the window and said, "We'll be quick. I...I just can't wait."

He knew the feeling. He'd never wanted anyone as badly as he wanted Marley, and yet there was more than just desire pulsing through his veins. Emotions he hadn't allowed himself to feel in years bubbled up to the surface. Tenderness and sorrow and something hot and painful he couldn't quite label.

His head lolled to the side as she stroked his stiff shaft, bringing him to a level of pleasure he'd never known before. Gulping, he met her gaze, and everything he felt was reflected right back at him.

"You're amazing," he said in a quiet voice.

Surprise and joy filled her face. Then she laughed. "You don't have to woo me with sweet words. I'm the one doing the seducing here, remember?"

"I'm not wooing." His voice cracked, much to his dismay. "I mean it, sweetheart, you're amazing. You're the strongest woman I've ever met." Caleb cupped her breasts through the fabric of her top, fondling them gently, then moved one hand down to her stomach. "And the sexiest."

A pretty flush rose on her cheeks. "Now you're talking crazy."

He slid his hand under her tank top. Circled her belly button with his index finger, then stroked his way between her legs. "No," he disagreed. "It's true. You're sexy, Marley, so unbelievably sexy."

She gasped when he pushed aside the crotch of her panties and began to prod and tease her damp folds. She was more than ready for him, but he toyed with her for a few more seconds, drawing a series of soft, anxious purrs from her throat. Finally, when he couldn't stand it any longer, he withdrew his finger, covered himself with the condom she produced from her purse, and thrust his cock inside her. They released simultaneous groans, pressing their foreheads against each other for a moment. And then Marley started to move.

She rode him furiously, while he dug his fingers into her waist and moved his hips to meet each frantic motion. Something primal unraveled inside him, a wild and inexplicable need to claim her, to push deep into her and show her it was where he belonged.

Where he *wanted* to belong.

"You're so beautiful," he muttered, watching the pleasure seep into her face.

She moaned again. Sagged into his chest and pressed her lips to his neck as she moved over him. Caleb wrapped his arms around her, drawing her closer. The feel of her full breasts crushed against his chest made his heart rate soar. He could feel her heart, too, thudding against his pecs. What was happening to him? This was more than sex...this was... Lord, he didn't even know what it was. He just knew that he never wanted it to end.

He growled when her teeth captured his earlobe, and gave a deep upward thrust that had his knees knocking against the steering wheel. It was a reminder of their surroundings, and he urged her to move faster, to send them both over the edge.

"Come for me, Marley." The words squeezed out between gasps. "Now, sweetheart."

Their joint release was fast, but oh, so sweet. An intense rush of pleasure spiraled through him, scorching his nerve endings, as Marley convulsed in his arms.

She whimpered as waves of orgasm rocked through her, and he held her tight, riding it out with her.

"Like I said," she murmured, her breath hot against his neck. "You turn me on hard and fast." She paused. "You called me sweetheart."

"I did?" When she nodded, he swallowed a lump of unease. "Oh. I'm sorry, I didn't mean to make you uncomf—"

"I liked it," she cut in. "It's the first term of endearment you've given me. It was...nice."

Nice? More like scary as hell. He'd called her sweetheart without even noticing it. He'd made love to her in a car, in public, where anyone could have walked up and ambushed them. Including Grier.

Oh, Christ, and he'd just mentally referred to what had happened between them as making love.

He was in deep, deep trouble.

Caleb stared at Marley as she gingerly climbed out of his lap and slipped back into her shorts. She looked happy and aroused and so outrageously beautiful his heart ached.

He couldn't tell her the truth. Not now.

He'd do it tomorrow.

Just one more night with her, that's all he wanted. One more night to hold her and kiss her and lose himself in the sweetness that poured out of her.

He'd tell her the truth tomorrow.

FOR THE SECOND MORNING in a row, Marley woke up with a smile on her face. Next to her, Caleb was sprawled on his stomach again, and a rush of pleasure flooded her as she admired his long, lean body. He was fully naked, and she couldn't take her eyes off his strong, back and firm ass.

Was it possible to want someone this much? They'd had sex numerous times yesterday, including a hot session at four in the morning, when Caleb had roused her from slumber with his tongue between her legs. Yet each time she looked at him, she craved him again.

A twinge of discomfort pulsed in her belly as she realized there was more than craving going on here. She was developing feelings for Caleb.

She hadn't wanted to analyze her actions of the past week, but it was getting hard not to. Having sex with him in a car, in broad daylight, was one thing, but bringing him home to meet her father? Strolling down the beach with him?

Those things had nothing to do with sex, and everything to do with...with what? A relationship?

She gulped. Well, why *shouldn't* she want a relationship with him? He was an amazing lover, a great listener. He was smart, he made her laugh with that subtle, dry humor of his. Heck, he could even cook, which he'd proved last night when he'd fixed dinner for the two of them.

Then again, Patrick had been all of those things, too.

She scowled. Damn Patrick. That man had broken something inside of her. He'd stolen her capacity for trust. Trust not only for others, but for herself.

Marley pushed aside the distressing thought, got out of bed and headed for the bathroom. When she came out, she rolled a pair of socks onto her feet and tied her hair up, while Caleb continued to sleep. He didn't look so peaceful this time, though. A crease marred his forehead, as if he were agonizing over something, even in slumber.

She contemplated giving him a wake-up call that

would surely vanquish his inner demons, but decided against it. They'd been up late; she ought to give him time to recover before ravishing his body again.

Grinning to herself, she walked downstairs and opened the front door to check the mail. Her postman, Ernie, made his deliveries impossibly early, and sure enough, stacks of envelopes cluttered her mailbox, probably sitting there since seven o'clock on the dot. A few doors down, she noticed her neighbor Kim rooting through her own mailbox. Marley knew the other woman had recently lost her husband, and she offered a gentle smile when the tall brunette spotted her. They waved at each other, then walked into their respective houses.

Marley took the stack of envelopes into the kitchen, flipping through them while she turned on the coffeemaker. She normally paid her bills online, but with Hernandez confiscating her laptop, she'd have to use telephone banking.

After pouring herself a cup of coffee, she sat at the kitchen table and began to go through the mail. Bill, junk, credit card promotion, bill, bank statement—her hand hesitated on the last envelope. She furrowed her brow in confusion. She'd opted for online statements for her checking account, and the statement for her savings account had arrived last week. Why was the bank sending her another statement?

Frowning, she dug her nail under the flap and sliced open the envelope. She pulled out the sheet of paper inside and went utterly still when she noticed Patrick's name underneath her own at the top of the statement.

She quickly scanned the information, then gasped.

Why on earth was there a hundred thousand dollars in an account that was supposed to be frozen?

10

STARING AT THE BANK STATEMENT, Marley rubbed her forehead for a moment, just in case the hours of sex she'd engaged in last night had exhausted her more than she'd thought. But when she looked down at the paper again, the transaction record remained the same.

Marley could barely breathe. Why had money been deposited? The cops had led her to believe the account would be frozen. Was it just a bank error, or was the tremor of fear skittering up her spine justified? Oh, God. Was Patrick moving drug money through the account?

She pushed her chair back with a loud scrape against the tiles. Still clutching the statement, she picked up the cordless phone from the kitchen counter and punched in the number of the bank with unsteady fingers.

At the automatic prompt, she keyed in the account number and her PIN, and waited, reminding herself to exhale. An operator came on the line surprisingly quickly, sparing her the awful tinny music every company and institution seemed to use for its hold function.

"This is Jennifer, how can I help you?" came a bubbly voice.

"Hi, Jennifer." Marley took a breath. "I'm just glancing over my recent bank statement and I noticed some inconsistencies."

"I can definitely look into that. I need to ask you a few security questions first."

Marley stifled a grumble as she went through the security process, offering her birth date, address and verifying the account information.

"So what seems to be the problem?" Jennifer asked after the CIA interrogation ended.

Marley's jaw tightened. "I'm seeing a deposit here, but I was under the impression the account was frozen."

"Hmm. Let me check your file. Can you hold?" Without waiting for a reply, Jennifer sent Marley into the land of elevator music.

She released the groan she'd been suppressing, wanting to kick something. What was going on? She'd dealt with banking errors before—usually a potential fraud issue where they canceled her ATM card, or an interest reversal—but a one-hundred-thousand dollar deposit in an account that was supposed to be inactive? This was one monster of an error.

Jennifer popped back on the line. "Ms. Kincaid?"

"I'm here."

"All right, so I noticed on your file that you opened the account with a…Mr. Patrick Neil Grier, is that correct?"

Marley gritted her teeth. "Yes."

"Well, the account is still active."

"I can see that." She sighed. "I'm just wondering why. What about the recent activity I'm seeing on this statement? Can you tell me where the deposit came from?"

"Sure thing. I need to ask you a few more security questions first."

Oh, for the love of God.

Jennifer rattled off another series of questions, just short of asking Marley for the name of the boy she'd lost her virginity to. And then chirped, "Let's take a look-see, shall we?"

Marley was beginning to seriously despise Jennifer.

"All right, I'm seeing a one-hundred-thousand-dollar wire transfer from a European cash office. Other than that, it's anonymous."

A rush of fury flooded her belly, causing her to tighten her fingers around the phone. Patrick was responsible for this. She knew it. He just couldn't stop messing around with her life, could he? He'd lied to her, disappeared on her and now he was throwing suspicion right back on her by moving money into an account that had her name on it. Hernandez would only see this as another sign of her guilt.

She wished Patrick were here, standing right in front of her, so she could strangle him with her bare hands.

"Is there anything else I can do for you today, Ms. Kincaid?" Jennifer chirped.

"No, you've done quite enough," Marley muttered. "Thanks."

She disconnected the call and resisted the urge to whip the phone across the kitchen. Okay. She had to calm down. And she had to call the police again. They'd obviously misled her by saying the account was inactive, and were probably sitting around at the station, taking bets on whether she would call it in when she discovered the deposit.

Hernandez would no doubt bet against her.

Good thing she wasn't going to give him that satisfaction.

"YOU SLEPT WITH HER. You damn idiot."

AJ's harsh voice was not one Caleb wanted greeting him so early in the morning, but at least Marley wasn't in the room to hear the angry words hissing out of the phone. He slid up in bed and leaned against the headboard, wiping the sleep from his eyes. The bathroom door was open, the light off, so he knew Marley must be downstairs, probably making breakfast.

Caleb opted for the avoidance route. "You're okay there by yourself, right? Getting enough sleep?"

His partner sounded incredulous. "Yes, Agent Ford, I'm sleeping just fine. I'm getting in twenty-minute cat-naps, and watching the monitors, one of which started shrieking last night when a stray dog walked past the porch motion sensor. I'm also eating my veggies and saying my prayers and all that fun stuff." AJ let out a loud curse. "Now how about we talk about you again. You know, about the fact that you *slept* with her."

Caleb drew in a breath. "I got caught up in...in the moment."

"Caught up in the moment?" Disbelief dripped from AJ's voice. "Look, I know you're having a ton of fun spending time with Nurse Hottie, but don't you ever forget why we're here, Caleb. This stakeout is about catching Grier, it's about Russ, not your goddamn libido."

Caleb closed his eyes. "I know."

There was a long silence on the other end.

"What?" Caleb asked. "Say whatever you're thinking."

"You don't want to hear it."

"Say it, AJ."

"Fine." His partner released a heavy breath. "I don't think you got caught up in the moment, man. I think you got caught up in *her*."

"What's that supposed to mean?"

"It means you've fallen in love with her, you moron."

The phone shook in his hand. Love? That was ridiculous.

Panic clutched at his chest like icy-cold fingers. No, he couldn't have fallen for her. So what if he liked being with her and making her laugh and seeing her bright smile when he woke up in the morning? So what if she made his body burn and amazed him with her constant optimism? So what?

It didn't mean he loved her, did it?

"You still there?"

AJ's tone was oddly gentle. It made Caleb's jaw tense. "Yeah, I'm here."

"You don't have a response to what I just said?"

He swallowed. "I have to tell her the truth, AJ."

"You can't do that."

"Why not?" he asked, running the fingers of one hand through his hair in frustration.

"Because if she *is* helping Grier, you'll tip her off, and then she'll tip him off."

"She's not helping Grier," he said through clenched teeth. "I know her, AJ. Like you said, I've been spending time with her, and I know in my gut she's not capable of that."

"Your gut isn't going to bring Russ back," AJ said.

"Nothing will bring Russ back." Caleb's chest squeezed with pain. "Russ is gone, and Grier is the one responsible for that. Not Marley."

AJ uttered another low expletive, but Caleb cut him off before he could object. "I can't lie to her anymore. I can't do it." A lump of grief lodged in his throat. "She trusts me. She *likes* me. And I feel like a total ass every time I look at her. I can't do this to her anymore."

Resignation lined AJ's tone. "And you still insist you're not in love with her, huh?" He paused. "Do what you want, Ford, I'm not going to stop you. But think real hard before ruining your cover. You don't want this blowing up in your face."

AJ hung up, and Caleb was left staring down at the phone. He wouldn't take his partner's advice, though. He *had* thought long and hard about it, and he knew in his heart that he couldn't lie about who he was any longer. He had to come clean, not just for Marley's sake, but for his own.

Getting out of bed, he slipped into his jeans and then searched for his T-shirt. He found it balled up on the floor and, with a sigh, pulled the wrinkled material over his head. After he used the bathroom and brushed his teeth, he headed downstairs. He found Marley sitting in the kitchen, staring at the half-painted wall. She still wore her pajamas, which consisted of tiny boxer shorts and a loose tank top, and she looked cute and fresh-faced as she sat there.

"No pancakes?" he teased.

At his question, her head popped up. She seemed confused for a moment, then she gave a dull shake of her head.

An alarm buzzed in his gut. With purposeful strides, he rounded the table, sank into the chair directly beside hers and cupped her delicate chin with his hands. "What happened?"

Without a word, she picked up a folded piece of

paper from the tabletop and handed it to him, looking tormented.

The bank logo immediately caught his eye. He scanned the details, realizing he was looking at the statement for the joint account she'd opened with Grier.

He pretended it was news to him. "What's this?"

"This," she said in a stiff voice, "is the account I opened with Patrick, which the cops told me was frozen." She snatched the paper from his hand and held it up as if it were laced with anthrax. "The account is still active, and he's putting money in it! Drug money, most likely. God, why can't the police just catch him already?"

Caleb rested his forehead in the palm of his hand.

"Why won't he stop haunting me?" Tears coated her dark lashes and her breath came in short gasps. "I'm so stupid. How did I fall for all his lies? I thought he was a good person."

A weight settled in Caleb's rib cage, causing his heart to constrict painfully. "He lied to you."

"Yeah, and I believed him. I was so wrong about him," she said, twisting her hands together. Then she swiped at her wet eyes. "I'm sorry. I didn't mean to dump all this on you."

He swallowed. "Don't apologize. You didn't do anything wrong."

"Hernandez isn't going to agree." She stared at him in dismay. "He's going to think I helped Patrick put the money in the account."

"You're going to call Hernandez?"

She looked surprised. "I have to. Obviously they lied and didn't freeze the account like they said they would. Or maybe it was the bank's mistake. Either way, I have to tell them. I'm going to do it in person, so hopefully

Hernandez will see I really didn't have anything to do with this."

"And if he doesn't believe you?"

"Then he doesn't believe me," she repeated in a flat voice. "I still have to let them know."

They already know.

Caleb drew a gulpful of air into his burning lungs. This was it. The time to tell her the truth. He opened his mouth, ready to do it, to bite the bullet and tell her he was a federal agent, but suddenly she placed her hand on his arm and said, "Will you come with me to the police station?"

He faltered. "You want me there?"

"I know it's a lot to ask, but I don't want to face him alone. Will you come?"

In a hoarse voice, he said, "Of course I will. But first I need to tell you—"

She cut him off with a desperate "Thank you" as she stumbled to her feet. "Let me just take a quick shower and then we can go."

Frustration rose inside of him. "Marley, wait—"

"You should go next door and change while I'm up-stairs," she interrupted, a faint smile on her lips as she studied his wrinkled shirt.

"I will, but first—"

"I'll meet you out front in fifteen minutes." And then she bounded out of the kitchen.

Caleb stared at the empty doorway, listening to the sound of her footsteps thudding up the stairs. Damn it, why hadn't she let him finish? He needed to tell her everything before they went to the police station—if she even desired his company after the truth came out.

With a sigh, he stood up, realizing the truth would yet again have to wait. Until Marley came out of the shower, anyway. The sigh became a discouraged groan, which he tamped down as he headed toward the front entrance.

Might as well go next door and change his damn shirt. At least then he wouldn't look like a slob while he faced her wrath.

MARLEY HAD JUST PEELED OFF her pajamas when a disconcerting flash of clarity sliced through her. What had she been thinking, asking Caleb to accompany her to the police station? She'd only been thinking about herself, she realized as she sagged against the bathroom wall.

She suddenly felt like kicking herself. God, talk about overdependent. As much as she'd appreciate having Caleb's support while she faced Hernandez, she knew she couldn't ask that of him. He'd already been present for the last confrontation with the detective, and they hadn't even known each other that well then. She didn't want to keep dragging him into this mess. It wasn't fair to Caleb. Patrick had been *her* mistake. And she was the only one who could fix it.

Anyway, she didn't want him to view her as some damsel in distress that he constantly needed to rescue. They'd just started seeing each other, for Pete's sake.

Drawing in a long breath, she left the bathroom and quickly got dressed. She would go next door and tell Caleb she needed to do this alone. He didn't deserve to spend his morning in a police station.

She hurried downstairs, slipped into her sneakers and flew out the front door, approaching the Strathorn house with determined strides.

On the porch, she opened the front door without bothering to ring the doorbell. She already knew Caleb was home, and considering he'd been staying at her house for the past two days, she hardly thought he'd mind if she let herself in.

"Caleb?" she called as she walked into the house.

His voice drifted down from upstairs. "I'll be down in a second."

He sounded strained, panicked even, but it wasn't his tone that made her freeze. When he'd spoken, she'd heard a clatter, as if he'd dropped something—but the expletive that had followed wasn't uttered by Caleb. The voice had been deeper, raspier.

An alarm bell went off in her head. As her palms grew damp, she approached the staircase and peered up. The second-floor hallway seemed to be empty. Did he have someone up there?

With wariness wrapping around her spine like strands of ivy, she climbed the stairs, reaching the second-floor landing just as Caleb popped out of the bedroom at the very end of the hall.

"Hey," he said, looking frazzled. "I was just getting dressed and—"

"Who's in there?" she cut in, narrowing her eyes.

He hesitated, only for a second, but it was hesitation just the same. "What? There's nobody here. I was—"

Marley brushed past him, unable to let go of the misgiving pulsing in her bloodstream. "I heard someone, Caleb."

She headed for the doorway he'd just exited, knowing she was probably being ridiculous but completely helpless to stop the sudden onslaught of suspicion. This was a total invasion of privacy. Maybe she hadn't heard another voice at all. Maybe she was—

She froze as she entered the bedroom.

Her hands dropped to her sides, her entire body

growing colder than a glacial ice cap. All the oxygen rushed from her lungs, leaving her breathless.

The room was empty, but that wasn't what shocked her to the core. Oh no, it was the computer monitors sitting on the long desk pushed up under the window. At least half a dozen of them. A couple had switched into screen-saver mode, but the rest... She stumbled forward. Oh, God. The rest displayed very clear images of her house.

Her front porch. Her backyard. Her kitchen. Her bedroom window.

Oh, God.

Bile rose in her throat. Caleb had been watching her.

But why? Why the hell would he— She stiffened again when her gaze landed on the photograph taped to one of the monitors.

Her pulse shrieked in her ears as she moved closer. As she looked at the photo and saw Patrick Grier's face peering back at her.

She stared at the picture for a very long time, fighting back wave after wave of nausea.

A noise came from behind, causing her to spin around and face Caleb.

Their gazes collided, and she stood there, watching all the color seep out of his face. Watching as a thick cloud of guilt settled over his blue eyes.

"Marley," he choked out.

Her fingers curled into two tight fists. "You son of a bitch."

11

MARLEY SWAYED AS ice slithered through her veins. Rage was the only thing that kept her feet rooted to the floor while her heart slapped against her ribcage, urging her to run.

Never breaking eye contact with Caleb, she forced her vocal cords to work. "Who are you?"

"I…" His Adam's apple bobbed as he swallowed. "I've been monitoring your house in case Patrick shows up."

"Patrick," she echoed.

"Yes. We suspected he might come to San Diego, so—"

"We?" she interrupted, anger continuing to claw its way up her spine. "Who's *we?*"

"The DEA… I'm a federal agent."

"A federal agent," she said, feeling her stomach roil.

"Yes."

Marley wished she could crawl into a hole and disappear. Her heart felt as though it was full of little razor blades. Each time it beat, a shudder of pain shot through her body. And each time she took a breath, her lungs burned.

How could he do this to her? She'd trusted him, and all the while he'd been lying to her.

Caleb squared his shoulders, sucking in a breath and releasing it.

"How long have you been here, watching me?" she demanded.

He held his ground as he looked straight into her eyes. "Two weeks."

Marley staggered backward. She couldn't believe this was happening. Two weeks! He'd been spying on her for the past two weeks, one of which he'd spent conning his way into her life. Into her *bed*.

She'd slept with him. She'd taken him to meet her family. She'd laughed with him and kissed him, and the whole time he was pretending to be someone else. Resentment coursed through her, trailed by humiliation. At the moment, she wasn't sure whom she was angrier with—him, for deceiving her, or herself, for falling for it again.

"Marley, I'm sorry," he said. "I'm sorry I didn't tell you the truth earlier, but…"

She scowled. "But what?"

"I wasn't supposed to make contact with you in the first place," he confessed. "I only did because I saw you hanging from the eaves, and I didn't want to let you fall."

"Why didn't you tell me then?"

"I couldn't." He looked at the ground. "There was always the chance that you were still involved with Grier, that you'd tip him off."

A breath flew out of her mouth. "Involved with… You thought I was a suspect?"

He shook his head. "Maybe a little, at first. But not now. I know you're not involved with any of Patrick's dealings, Marley."

She glared at him. "How nice for me! The man who slept with me under false pretenses didn't think I was a criminal. I feel so much better." She clenched her fingers. "So, do you have sex with all your potential suspects, or am I the only one?"

He winced. "I have never gotten involved with a witness before," he said, emphasizing the word *witness*.

She shot him a cold look. "Lucky me."

"I was desperate. My best friend was killed in that raid, and the person who murdered him is out there somewhere, going unpunished. I didn't mean to get involved with you...it just happened...and I've been torn up in knots about lying to you."

"I'm sorry about your friend, but there were other ways you could have handled this." Her voice wobbled. "Telling me the truth would have been a good start."

"I wanted to, really." His claim meant little in light of his actions.

"What exactly have you been doing, Caleb?"

He hesitated. "Watching."

"Are you recording everything?"

"Yes."

"Recording everything," she whispered, remembering all the special moments they'd shared. Moments she'd thought were private. "God, I can't believe this."

CALEB STOOD PARALYZED as he watched Marley's feelings for him die.

Her shoulders were stiff as she turned and made a move for the bedroom door. "You're a bastard, Caleb."

"Marley, wait."

He tried to grab hold of her arm, but she shrugged him off as if she'd been stung by a scorpion. "Don't you dare touch me. You've been lying to me since the moment we met. I was always just a case for you. So don't you ever touch me again, do you hear me, *Agent* Ford?"

"Damn it, Marley, you're more than a case."

She stared through him. "Right."

"It's true." His heart twisted in his chest. "Something happened once we got involved. I started to care about you."

"You don't care about me," she said coldly. "You're just trying to butter me up with sweet words so I'll forget about all the lies."

"I'm not lying about this. And believe me, I'm not sure I even like it. My job has always been the most important thing in my life. I never wanted anything more than that. But then I met you, and now...now I realize what I've been missing all these years."

Marley moved toward the door again.

"A job isn't going to keep me warm at night, or make me laugh the way you do," Caleb continued in a soft voice. "A job isn't going to make me pancakes or seduce me in a car. Being with you has shown me that it's okay to open up to another person."

"Looks like you're going to have to be satisfied with the job." Marley stumbled to the door, tears coating her thick eyelashes.

"Marley, please," he burst out.

She turned around and paused in the doorway, slowly meeting his eyes. "I will never forgive you for this," she murmured.

Then she marched out of the room.

"Well," AJ's dry voice sounded from the bathroom

he'd ducked into when they'd spotted Marley's brisk walk next door on the monitors. "That was unpleasant."

Ignoring his partner, Caleb stared at the doorway for a second, then tore out of it. He heard the front door slam as he hurried down the stairs, but he kept going. He couldn't let it end like this. Every word he'd uttered up in the bedroom had been true. He *did* care about her. He'd told her things about himself that he'd never told another soul. His life in foster care, his mother's overdose, how hard it was to talk about his feelings. He couldn't lose her now, not when he'd finally found someone he actually wanted in his life.

He caught up to her on the front lawn at the same time a blue pickup truck came to a stop in her driveway. He bit back a groan when he saw Marley's brother slide out of the driver's side, pulling a tool belt from the passenger seat.

"Marley!" Caleb called after her.

She quickly ascended the porch steps. Sam must have noticed the anger radiating off his sister's body, because he darted toward them, reaching the porch just as Caleb did.

"What's going on here?" Sam asked, looking wary.

"Nothing," Marley answered. She avoided Caleb's face and glanced at her brother. "Come in, let's work on that closet."

"Marley, please," Caleb said. "Just let me explain."

"You've done all the explaining you need to."

"We can't leave things like this."

"Oh, yes, we can."

Sam's eyes moved back and forth between the two of them. He opened his mouth to speak again, but Marley raised her hand and gestured for him to come inside. "Agent Ford was just leaving."

Sam wrinkled his forehead, then walked up the steps and followed his sister into the house. "Agent Ford?" Caleb heard Sam say, and then the door shut behind them.

Caleb stood there feeling frustrated. He wanted to knock on the door, or hell, kick it open and try to make Marley understand, but he knew she wasn't in the frame of mind to listen right now. He'd blown it. She would never forgive him for this, and at the moment, he didn't particularly blame her.

His shoulders slumped. Slowly, he walked back next door and headed upstairs. When he entered the bedroom, AJ was at the desk, looking a little shell-shocked.

It killed him to do it, but Caleb turned to the monitors. He saw Marley lead her brother into the kitchen, where they sat down at the table. Sam leaned forward. Marley's eyes flashed as she filled her brother in on what had just happened. Sam's face hardened, and he tried to get up, but Marley forced him to sit back down.

He's not worth it, he could almost hear her say.

He hoped that one day he'd be able to convince her otherwise.

He tore his gaze from the screen, noticing that AJ was tentatively holding out a green folder to him. "What's that?" Caleb muttered.

"Hernandez's file. Lukas from headquarters faxed it over." AJ paused. "Read it. It might take your mind off…you know."

Caleb took the folder, but rather than reading it, he set it on the desk and walked over to the bed. He dropped onto the mattress, feeling beaten and battered.

Ravaged. The way he'd felt the night of the warehouse raid, as he held his dying best friend in his arms.

But this time, there was nobody to direct all that grief and anger at. Grier had killed Russ, but Caleb was the one responsible for bringing the anguish into Marley's eyes.

"Caleb...look, you were just doing your job," AJ said.

Caleb stared at his friend. "No, I wasn't. My job didn't require me to befriend her. Or to sleep with her."

"She'll forgive you."

"No, she won't."

Why would she? He'd screwed up big-time. Taken Marley's trust and whipped it out the window, along with his own code of honor.

"HE'S A COP?" GWEN EXCLAIMED later that evening, ten minutes before their shift was scheduled to begin.

Marley sat down on the bench with a weak nod.

Gwen shook her head, her eyes wide. "A *cop?*"

"Yes," Marley said gloomily.

"And he only got close to you to find Patrick?"

"Yep, but apparently he developed feelings for me along the way." Right. He'd been spying on her for weeks, yet he expected her to believe that he gave a damn?

She suddenly wished she'd called in sick. She'd spent the entire day stewing over Caleb's lies. Berating herself for being such an idiot and yet again placing her trust in the wrong man. Sam had wanted to stick around, even tried distracting her by saying they should work on the hall closet together, but she'd ended up sending him away. She couldn't bear seeing the pity on her brother's face.

Caleb's betrayal continued to haunt her. It pulsed through her veins and buzzed in her mind and pretty much made it impossible to focus on anything else. She'd come into work only because she needed a diversion from her thoughts.

"I can't believe this," Gwen said.

Marley's lips tightened. "Neither can I. I thought he actually cared about me."

Gwen tied the drawstring of her scrubs and stepped toward Marley, gently touching her arm. "Maybe he does, Mar. It might have been a case for him at first, but that could have changed."

"That's what he claims, but why should I believe him? He's lied to me about everything, Gwen."

Gwen looked thoughtful.

"Maybe you should talk to him again, try to make some sense of all this."

"Sense of it? He *lied* to me."

"He lied about what he did for a living," Gwen clarified. "That doesn't mean he lied about how he feels for you."

Marley fell silent. She thought about the times they'd had sex, the emotion overflowing in his blue eyes as he'd held her tightly, as he'd told her she was beautiful. She hadn't picked up on anything insincere in those actions, in those words, but how could she trust her own judgment after being duped. Twice.

"I don't know." She rubbed her forehead in frustration. "I keep thinking about all the time we spent together. It felt real, Gwen."

"Maybe it was."

"The way things were so real with Patrick?" she retorted.

"Patrick was a soulless jerk who dealt drugs and

killed people. Caleb is a cop. A drug-enforcement cop, to boot." Gwen sounded conflicted, a deep crease in her forehead. "He cleans up the streets, tries to make them safe—does that make him a bad man?"

"He *lied*," Marley said through clenched teeth. She took a breath. "Whatever, it was just a fling and it's over. I'll just have to deal with it, the way I dealt with everything that happened with Patrick."

Her friend sat down next to her and took her hand. Squeezing her fingers, Gwen searched Marley's face, a perceptive glimmer in her eyes. "What are you really angry about, hon? Because if it really was just a fling, you wouldn't care this much. You'd just chalk it up as another stupid mistake, the way it was with, what's his name, the guy you went out with before Patrick."

"Brad," she murmured.

"Right, Brad. He was a total ass, remember? He stood you up on your birthday."

Marley sighed. "I really pick winners, don't I?"

"You're missing the point," Gwen said with a sigh of her own. "I'm just saying, some men are jerks. Brad was, and you barely blinked after you dumped him."

"And Patrick? Are you saying I shouldn't have been furious about *him?*"

"No, I'm not saying that. Patrick is different. You were with him for five months. You lived together. Of course you should have been furious. But you've only known Caleb a week. It's normal to be angry, sure, but not devastated." Gwen hesitated. "Unless you care about him more than you're willing to admit."

Marley smothered another sigh. "I…liked being with him," she finally admitted. "He's such a hard man to get to know, hardly ever talks about his feelings, but I thought he was starting to open up to me."

She swallowed. "And when we had sex, I felt really... connected to him."

"Then you need to talk to him again," Gwen advised. "You need to find out if he felt that connection, too."

"I don't know. I just don't know."

She thought about Caleb's confession, the regret flickering in his eyes, and for a moment she experienced a pang of doubt. But then the memory of all those computer monitors pushed its way into the forefront of her brain, and the doubt transformed into anger again. She imagined Caleb sitting at that computer desk, watching her, talking about her, wondering if she was helping Patrick leave the country.

How could she ever trust him again?

Her mind was spinning, but considering she was about to start her shift, she couldn't afford to be distracted.

Taking a breath, she stood up and said, "I can't talk about this anymore. I need to worry about my patients right now."

"Just promise you'll think about what I said," Gwen said.

"Sure," Marley said, then kicked off her sandals. Determined to change for work, tend to her patients and forget all about Caleb and Patrick and every other headache pulsing through her mind, she walked to her locker and opened the door.

"Oh, my God," she choked out.

"What?" Gwen rushed to her side, sucking in a gasp when she saw what Marley was looking at.

On the inside of the metal door, scrawled in the red lipstick she kept on the top shelf, was the word *Whore*.

And underneath it, attached with a piece of silver duct tape, was a photograph of Marley.

A photograph she recognized as the one Patrick used to keep in his wallet.

A photograph that now featured a big black X directly over her face.

12

TWO HOURS LATER, MARLEY SAT on her living-room couch, stiff as a board, unable to erase the memory of Patrick's vile message. She and Gwen had called the police immediately, and officers had turned the nurses' locker room into a crime scene, dusting Marley's locker for fingerprints and questioning everyone who'd been working on the floor that day. So far, none of the hospital staff had admitted to seeing Patrick.

She fought a wave of nausea as she pictured what had happened. He'd waltzed into her place of work, strolled into the locker room. Opened her locker. Touched her things. She wanted to throw up just thinking about it. Was he fearless, or just crazy?

Crazy, obviously. And apparently enraged. She shivered and wondered what on earth she'd done to earn Patrick's rage. The disgusting message was so different from the sweet email he'd sent only days ago. Something had changed during that time, something had infuriated Patrick so much that he'd decided to paint a target on her.

Fortunately, the police had decided to take this

matter seriously. Her house was swarming with law-enforcement officers. Hernandez was in the armchair next to the couch, a notepad in his hand so he could take her statement. Three other officers from the SDPD hovered behind him, while three DEA agents, including Caleb and his partner, stood near the door. Caleb's partner had introduced himself as AJ Callaghan, and Marley had been angry just shaking his hand, especially when she learned he'd been next door with Caleb this entire time.

Caleb had reacted with a brief flash of guilt during the introduction with AJ, but now he leaned against the bookshelf, his face completely expressionless.

She couldn't bring herself to look at him for more than a few seconds. He wore a long-sleeved black shirt and snug black trousers. The butt of a gun poked out of the holster on his hip. The weapon was a reminder of his true identity.

He hadn't said a word to her since entering the house, but concern creased his handsome features.

How concerned had he been when he'd slept with her while pretending to be someone else?

She shoved aside the bitter thought and focused on Hernandez's latest question. "It's the picture from his wallet," she said for the second time. "I gave it to him a few days after he proposed. You can tell from the creases that it was folded a few times to fit somewhere small."

Hernandez jotted a note, then looked up at her with hard eyes. "And you say the locker was that way when you opened it?"

"Yes." She gritted her teeth, wondering how many times she'd have to answer the same questions. "My last shift was yesterday morning, and I didn't go back to the hospital until eight o'clock tonight. When I left yesterday, my locker looked normal."

Hernandez made a harsh sound under his breath. Annoyance pricked at her skin like tiny little needles. For the love of God. What would it take to convince this man she was innocent, that *she* was the victim?

She opened her mouth to ask him just that, only to be interrupted by Caleb's husky voice. "Detective Hernandez?" he called from behind. "May I speak to you for a moment?"

Looking irritated, Hernandez excused himself and made his way over to Caleb. As Marley watched, the two men went out into the hall, heads bent together, voices low. Whatever Caleb had to say, the detective didn't like it. She could tell from the way his thick black eyebrows bunched together. Then Hernandez looked at the ground and his shoulders slumped.

What was Caleb saying? Whatever it was must have worked, because when Hernandez returned, his normally frosty tone had thawed considerably.

"Ms. Kincaid, do you have any idea what this message means?"

"I'm pretty sure he thinks I'm a whore," she said dryly.

"Yes, but do you know why he might think that? Do you have a new boyfriend?"

She forced herself not to glance over at Caleb. "No."

"Are you casually seeing anyone?"

She hesitated. "I did have a date two nights ago."

Hernandez leaned forward. "Where did you go on the date, which restaurant? Perhaps Grier saw you with another man and—"

"We didn't go out," she cut in. "We stayed in and ordered take-out."

For a moment she was tempted to stand up, point directly at Caleb, and yell, "It was him! We slept together that night, too."

Instinctively, she knew to keep her mouth shut. It wouldn't look good for Caleb if she announced his involvement with her. But she wasn't simply covering for him. The truth made her look like a total idiot, and she was tired of Hernandez glaring at her with that belittling and antagonistic expression.

Right now, he just looked disappointed. "You stayed in," he repeated. "Okay, well, my gut tells me Grier knows about that date, Ms. Kincaid. Somehow, he heard about it, or maybe—"

"He's close by," Caleb stated.

The room fell quiet at his words. Hernandez turned to Caleb. "You think so?"

Confidence lined Caleb's face. "He has to be. We know from the email that he had planned to reunite with Marley soon, and he's smart. He wouldn't risk walking up to her door, not unless he knew for sure what the law-enforcement situation was."

"He'd need to scout the area first," Hernandez agreed.

"I think he's doing more than that. He's watching her. He knows she had another man over—" there was a slight crack in Caleb's voice "—and in order to see that, he had to be close."

A tremor ran along Marley's skin. The notion that Patrick was lurking outside somewhere, watching her, was too frightening to contemplate. God, would she ever be rid of that man? She wished she'd never gone into his hospital room all those months ago, never agreed to that first date, never opened her heart to him.

"Okay, he can't be next door, since AJ and I have

occupied that space," Caleb said in a brisk voice. He glanced at Marley. "How well do you know your other neighbors?"

Since he'd spoken to her directly, she had no choice but to meet his eyes. Damn. Why did he have to be so attractive? Her heart shouldn't skip a beat anymore when she looked at him.

"Don and Melinda live in the house on the other side of mine," she answered. "They have three kids, but they're all away at camp for the summer. Next to them is Kim, she's a widow." She racked her brain for more names and faces. "Across the street is Mrs. White, she lives alone, kind of grumpy all the time but she can be sweet. I'm not sure about anyone else."

"Do you know if any of the ones you mentioned are on vacation, like the Strathorns?" Caleb asked.

"I don't think so. I saw Don and his wife the other day, and I saw Kim yesterday when I checked the mail." She paused. "I haven't seen Mrs. White in a few days, come to think of it, but she hardly ever leaves the house."

Caleb and the other men sprang to action before she even finished talking. She tried to hide her admiration as she watched Caleb bark orders at everyone. "We canvass each house one by one, only the ones that have a direct visual on Marley's. Teams of two. Hernandez, you're with me. Officer Thompson," he said to the thin, uniformed blond man, "you stay with Ms. Kincaid. Radio us if there are any disturbances."

"Yes, sir."

Marley's chest tightened with alarm as Caleb and the others unholstered their weapons. What if they got hurt? What if Caleb got hurt? She wanted to urge him to be careful, but clamped her mouth shut. She refused to let herself feel anything for him. Besides, he was a trained government agent. He could handle himself.

Still, her heart thudded as she watched him disappear through the doorway, his strides long and determined.

Please don't let him get hurt.

CALEB CROUCHED BESIDE the tall hedges of Lydia White's two-story Victorian home, silently gesturing for Hernandez to take the back. AJ and the other agents, as well as two of Hernandez's men, were already approaching the other houses in the vicinity, moving stealthily in the shadows.

With adrenaline coursing through his blood, Caleb held his Glock in his right hand and the radio in his left. He crept to the front door while Hernandez circled the house. As he reached the porch, his radio crackled and AJ's voice came through. "Kim just let us in. Preparing to search the house."

The radio went silent. Caleb stood in front of Lydia White's door and rapped his knuckles on it. There was no doorbell, just a sign on the mailbox that said No Solicitors. He knocked again, but still no answer.

"Lydia White?" he shouted. "This is Agent Caleb Ford with the Drug Enforcement Agency."

Nothing.

The radio came to life again. "Kim's house is clear." A moment later, one of Hernandez's officers checked in. "Don and Melinda Levenstein's house is clear."

"Lydia White," he said again. "With your permission, I'd like to search your house. There is a possible fugitive on the premises."

He debated picking the lock when static hissed out

from the radio. "Back-door lock's been jimmied open," came Hernandez's grim voice. "I'm going in."

The adrenaline in his veins flowed harder. No time to pick a lock. Instead, he kicked Lydia White's door open with his heavy black boot and then he was in the front hall, shrouded by darkness. Holding his weapon, he moved through the shadows, clearing the living room and a small den, before rendezvousing with Hernandez in the hallway.

"Kitchen's clear," the detective murmured.

The two men headed for the staircase, Hernandez falling into step behind Caleb, letting him take the lead. You could say a lot of things about Hernandez, but Caleb felt good knowing the detective had his back. The two of them moved together as if they'd been a team for years, scouting the hallway, using hand signals to direct their movements. They found the bathroom and master bedroom empty, then crept down the carpeted hall toward the single door at the end of it.

Caleb's instincts began to hum, growing stronger when a muffled sound broke through the silence.

He signaled for Hernandez to pull back. They paused in front of the white door, exchanging a significant look. Someone was in there. Slowly, Caleb rested his hand on the door handle, glanced at the other man again, then pushed his way into the room, weapon drawn.

A strangled cry came from the bed.

Caleb's eyes adjusted to the darkness, a soft curse exiting his mouth as he stared at the elderly woman bound and gagged on the bed. Had to be Lydia White.

Caleb held up his hand to silence the crying woman, scanning the bedroom. There was a door, ajar, at one end of the room. Hernandez slipped toward it, then kicked it open and yelled, "San Diego Police Department!"

Nobody was in there. After examining the narrow closet, Hernandez stepped back and said, "Clear."

Disappointment tightened Caleb's chest. Damn it. Grier had been here, and for a while, judging by the empty food containers littering the carpet.

Caleb went to the woman's side, pulling off her duct-tape gag as gently as he could. "Lydia White?"

"Yes," the woman croaked. "Oh, thank heavens you're here! He was going to kill me!"

Caleb helped her into a sitting position. He pulled the knife from the holster on his ankle and quickly sliced open the tape binding her hands and feet together. Holding it by the corners, he set the pieces of tape on the table next to the bed for forensics to print and bag. He knew without a doubt whose prints they'd find on the tape, all over the room, in fact.

That son of a bitch had been here, scheming and watching Marley. Caleb's eyes drifted to the window, then narrowed at the hole in the wall beside it. His pupils contracted as Hernandez flicked on the light, but adjusted quickly, and he noticed flecks of blood on the plaster where the drywall had been broken. Grier's DNA would be on it.

"Mrs. White, can you identify the man who did this to you?" Caleb asked.

She nodded, a soft sob sliding from her mouth. "Yes, yes, I'll never be able to forget that face."

"I know you've been through quite an ordeal," he said, keeping his tone quiet. Behind him, he heard Hernandez barking into the radio, arranging for a forensics team and an ambulance. "We're going to take you to the hospital, to get you checked out, all right?"

The elderly woman's eyes filled with tears. "It was so terrible, officer," she said in the raspy voice usually heard from long-time smokers. "He was here for that dear girl across the street. He was so angry!"

"Don't worry, Ms. Kincaid is under police protection. You are, too, now," Caleb assured her. "Mrs. White," he continued, "the man who did this to you— did he say he would be coming back? Did he give any indication of where he might have gone?"

"No. No, nothing," Lydia stated.

Caleb turned to Hernandez, who carefully walked through the bedroom, making sure not to touch anything. "Miguel, can you stay with Mrs. White while I go across the street to Kincaid's?"

Hernandez nodded, taking Caleb's place at Lydia's bedside, offering surprising words of comfort as he reassured her the paramedics would be there soon to examine her.

But Caleb wasn't worried about Lydia White as he left the house. The elderly woman was dehydrated and in shock, but she would be fine. Marley, on the other hand…

His chest constricted as he realized how close Grier had been this entire time. He bit the inside of his lip so hard he could taste the blood in his mouth. Christ, he was scared for her. He'd seen the digital photo one of Hernandez's men had taken of Marley's locker at the hospital, the thick black X marking her face in that picture.

He couldn't let Grier hurt Marley.

Swallowing hard, he ignored the sharp metallic taste and walked faster. When he marched into Marley's living room, she was still on the couch, her hands clasped in her lap. Officer Thompson stood by the window, watching the scene outside.

"Is the old lady all right?" the young officer inquired.

"She'll be fine. Thompson, do me a favor and excuse us for a moment."

With a nod, the officer left the room. Caleb heard the front door open and shut, then Thompson's footsteps as he descended the porch steps to help out the others.

"You have to listen to me right now," he began, his throat tight as he looked into her gorgeous eyes. "I know you're angry with me, and I don't blame you for that, but please, Marley, just hear me out."

"Okay," she said softly.

"I need you to understand how much danger you're in." An eddy of fear swirled in his stomach but he ignored it, trying to remain calm as he laid it all out in front of her. "When I first moved in next door, I suspected Patrick would come back for you. Not to hurt you, but to convince you to leave town with him, or maybe just to say goodbye. I suspected he was obsessed with you, and when he sent that email, I knew it was a matter of time before love, or infatuation—whatever you want to call it—pushed him to see you."

Marley unclasped her hands and pressed them on her knees. "And now?"

"Now he wants to hurt you." He sank into the armchair Hernandez had occupied earlier. "He was across the street for who knows how long, and he must have seen us together. He also has to know I'm with the DEA, because he saw me there during the warehouse raid."

"So he thinks I'm working with the cops."

"Or at the very least, sleeping with one." He flinched when he saw her eyes darken. "What he did to your locker was an act of violence, and it's an indication of what he wants to do to you."

"I know." Her bottom lip quivered. "I know the danger, Caleb. I can feel it. Where are you going with this?"

"Someone needs to stay here in the house with you," he said. "And I'd really appreciate it if you wouldn't object. You need protection."

"Okay," she said without any argument.

"Though I'd prefer it if you'd agree to stay in a safe house," he added.

Bitterness flickered across her face. "I'm not leaving my house, Caleb. Patrick has already turned my entire life upside down. I won't let him chase me from my home."

He'd known she'd say something like that. "Then an agent will stay here. Grier is going to find out what happened tonight. We might get lucky and he'll waltz back to White's house, unaware that we found his hideout, but I'm not holding my breath. He was probably in the area, saw the police activity and took off."

"So search the neighborhood," Marley burst out, sounding frustrated.

"We are. Units are combing the area as we speak, though my gut tells me Grier will be long gone by now."

"But he'll be back."

"He'll be back," Caleb echoed. "He might consider it too risky to come to this house, but he'll find a way to get to you, Marley. I'm certain of that."

She released a shaky breath and turned her head away, but not before he saw tears forming in the corners of her eyes. He wanted so badly to pull her into his arms and comfort her, but he knew she wouldn't allow it.

"You probably shouldn't go into work for a while," he continued. "It'll be too hard to protect you there, and today Grier showed us that he can find a way into the hospital without getting caught."

Marley's jaw tightened. "So I'm just supposed to sit around and wait for him to kill me?"

"He won't kill you." Caleb's pulse sped up at the mere thought. "I won't let him."

She fell quiet for a few long moments, then cleared her throat. "It can't be you, Caleb."

"What can't be me?"

"The agent who stays here. I don't want it to be you. Or your partner for that matter."

Something shifted in his chest. There, his heart had officially cracked in two. He wanted nothing more than to stay here with her, to protect this beautiful, generous woman who had once trusted him so willingly—and so misguidedly. It killed him that she didn't want him around, though he understood perfectly why that was.

But God, he wished she would trust him now, to protect her, at least. He'd still be next door, but what if that wasn't close enough? What if he wasn't fast enough?

His palms began to sweat and he rubbed them on the front of his pants. "No," he finally said, his voice sounding hoarse even to his own ears. "I'm not going anywhere. I'm not leaving you, Marley."

THE SHRIEK OF SIRENS reverberated in the night, causing Patrick to sink farther into the bushes. He'd been hunkered down in the small park directly behind Marley's cul-de-sac for the past hour, ever since he'd heard that first siren wail in the distance. Seconds from hopping the fence at the edge of the park, he'd been forced to retreat, and now he hid, waiting for the opportunity to get the hell out of here. Evidently the cops had discovered his hiding place, which sent a rush of fury to his gut.

A flash of color caught his eye, and he peeked out to see a cop car cruising along the street in front of the park. Patrols. They were obviously casing the entire neighborhood.

"Damn it," he muttered, ducking into the bushes again.

What was he supposed to do now? He'd planned on going for the money tonight. The black backpack slung over his shoulder contained the syringes and sedatives he'd stolen from the hospital earlier this afternoon. He still couldn't believe he'd walked in undetected and managed to break into one of the medicine cabinets. Managed to leave Marley a nice little message, too.

Now his plans were shot to hell. It could've been so easy. Break into the house next door to Marley's and stick a needle in that cop bastard's throat before he knew what hit him. And then, with the cop in a drug-induced slumber, Patrick would get his money from Marley's bathroom while she worked the night shift. He'd considered going back to the hospital after that, waiting outside in the parking lot for her to come out. Even contemplated forgiving her for sleeping around on him. God knows, starting a new life would be a lot more fun if he had someone with him.

But now...now everything had changed.

He peered out again, breathing a sigh of relief when he noticed the cruiser had disappeared. He needed to make a run for it. If the patrols turned up nothing, the cops might start searching the area on foot soon, and he couldn't afford to stay in this damn park all night.

He crept out of the bushes and stayed in the shadows, using the oak trees for cover, his guard on high alert with each careful step. Rocks lined the edge of the playground. He bent to pick up a decent-size one, then kept moving. He neared the sidewalk, his gaze darting up and down the street, and finally he zeroed in on a beat-up old Toyota with rust coating the doors. There was no telltale flash of an alarm as he approached the decrepit vehicle. Perfect car to hotwire.

Fingers tightening over the rock, he glanced around the dark, deserted street, then smashed in the driver's-side window and held his breath. No alarm sounded.

He was in business.

Rapidly, he opened the door and slid into the car, his hand reaching under the dash and yanking out a bundle of wires. Two minutes later, the engine rumbled and Patrick sped away as if his life depended on it.

Because it kind of did.

He drove fast. His breath came out in sharp puffs, growing steadier the farther he got from Marley's neighborhood. He glanced in the rearview mirror every two seconds, but no police cruisers appeared behind him. No flashing lights. No sirens.

Relief pounded into him. Shit. That had been close. Too close.

When he decided he was far enough away—he'd driven for a good half hour—he pulled up at the curb in front of a small strip mall and let the car idle.

Then he slammed his hands against the steering wheel in fury.

Damn it. What the hell was he supposed to do? He needed that money.

Then you're just going to have to get her to bring it to you.

A slow smile stretched across his mouth. Yeah. Yeah, that could work. Marley would have to bring him the money. But how? How could he get her to— He straightened his shoulders, the smile widening.

And just like that, he knew exactly what he needed to do.

13

MARLEY LIFTED HER HEAD in surprise. Caleb stood in front of her, his broad shoulders squared, his defiant expression making it clear he would not back down.

"I know you're angry with me," he began. "And you should be. I lied to you, and I abused your trust. But the only thing I lied about was what I do for a living. Everything else was real, Marley."

"Forgive me if I have a little trouble believing that," she replied.

"It's true. I'm still the same person. I never lied about my background. I never hid my personality." His voice grew wry. "Don't you think, if I was playing a part, I'd choose to be someone more charming, more likable? I know I'm flawed, Marley. I'm rough around the edges, I'm too serious, too intense, too…broken."

Her heart squeezed in her chest. No, she would not allow herself to be swayed by his words, no matter how earnest they sounded.

"That could have been part of the act," she said, wincing at the feeble pitch in her tone. "Make yourself out to be…to be *broken* so I'd feel some silly urge to fix you. You knew I was a nurse, that my job means I like to help people. Maybe you wanted me to help you."

"Remember when you told me it's okay to talk about things that hurt you? Well, for me, it's never been okay. Do you think I liked telling you about the day I found my mother overdosed on the floor? That it was all part of some sick game? I've never told anyone about that before." Caleb made a frustrated sound in the back of his throat. "I didn't plan on opening up to you, Marley. It just happened."

"Yeah, it conveniently happened."

He flinched at her harsh retort, but the determination on his face never wavered. "I won't leave you. Grier will try to get to you, but I refuse to let him. Did Hernandez tell you what happened to the last woman who got involved with Grier?"

She nodded, unable to speak.

"Well, I won't let that happen to you. You can be angry with me all you like—you can hate me if you want—but I'm not leaving this house. If I left and something happened to you…" Agony clung to his husky voice. "I'd never forgive myself. No matter what you believe, I care about you, and I'm staying right here to protect you."

She tried to ignore the rush of warmth that heated her belly. There wasn't a single false note in his heartfelt words. Was Gwen right? Was it possible Caleb truly did care for her? Patrick had covered up the fact that he was a criminal, had lied about his very nature. But Caleb was a cop, a man who'd sworn an oath to protect others, and now he was determined to protect her. If anything, that made him honorable, but did it excuse the lie he'd told her?

She sucked in a slow breath. "Caleb—"

"I'm not going anywhere," he interrupted, jutting out his chin. "Even if I have to sit on the front porch all night, even if I have to stand on a ladder outside your bedroom window, I won't leave."

As if a higher power were eavesdropping on their discussion, a loud crack of thunder sounded from outside. Seconds later, rain poured from the sky, pounding against the house. Marley turned to the window in disbelief, watching as raindrops streaked down the glass.

"I swear, you planned this," she grumbled, shaking her head at him. "Now I'll spend the whole night picturing you getting soaked on the porch, or struck by lightning while standing on a ladder."

His lips twitched, but he didn't say a word.

"Fine," she said. "You can stay. But this doesn't mean I forgive you, Caleb."

"I know."

They stared at each other for one long moment, and a kaleidoscope of emotions spun around in her body. A part of her wanted to break the distance between them and find solace in his strong arms. She wanted to feel his firm lips pressed against hers, his dark stubble scraping her cheek. But then there was the other part of her—the angry part—that looked at him and remembered the cameras next door.

The sound of the front door opening interrupted her thoughts. Her pulse quickened, as a feeling of foreboding shot up her spine. She'd been on edge ever since the incident with her locker, and she found herself jumping at shadows, startling at the merest sound. She kept expecting Patrick to pop out of a closet or blaze into the house with a gun.

Her heartbeat slowed when Caleb's partner appeared

in the doorway, shaking out his clothing and sending water droplets onto her parquet floor.

"Hernandez left for the hospital to get Mrs. White's statement," AJ said. "The other officers from the SDPD are continuing the patrols, and our guys are setting up posts around the neighboring houses. Are we heading next door?"

Caleb shook his head. "I'm staying here."

His partner's eyes flickered with surprise. "All right."

"Keep your radio on, and your eyes on the monitors," Caleb said brusquely. "If Grier decides to come back tonight, we're going to see him."

With a nod, AJ bid an awkward goodbye and left the room. Caleb walked him out, and she heard the metallic scrape of the lock sliding into place. He returned a few seconds later and said, "You should go up to bed. It's past midnight."

Marley was quite aware of the fact that they were now completely alone. The same way they'd been alone last night, when they'd made love for hours in her bedroom. A traitorous flame of desire licked at her skin.

No. No way. She couldn't let herself be tempted by this man. No matter how gorgeous he looked in his all-black get-up, with his dark hair falling onto his proud forehead.

She stumbled to her feet. "Yeah, I should go upstairs."

To her dismay, he followed, trailing after her as she climbed the stairs to the second floor. "I guess you can sleep in the guest room," she offered, gesturing to the doorway across from hers.

He shook his head. "I'll stay outside your door."

Annoyance tickled her throat. "For the love of—"

"I'll be right here if you need me," Caleb cut in. "Now stop arguing and go to bed."

She rolled her eyes. Fine, if he wanted to be all macho about this, she would let him. So what if he chose to sit on an uncomfortable hardwood floor all night? That was his problem.

The first thing she did after she walked into her bedroom and shut the door was make a beeline for the window. She closed the drapes, her lips thinning as she pictured Caleb's scary partner next door, watching her on the monitor. She fought the urge to give him a big fat scowl. Instead, she took the higher road and turned away from the window, heading to the bathroom to get ready for bed.

Ten minutes later, she slipped under the covers and stared up at the ceiling. Outside, the rain continued to pound against the house, drumming out a staccato beat on the roof.

Sleep did not come. She was too keyed up and afraid, unable to erase the memory of what Patrick had done to her locker. That angry red word, designed to scare, to accuse. She pushed the image from her mind, only to have it replaced with one equally disturbing—Caleb sitting outside her door. He was actually prepared to spend the night there. In the morning, his back would be throbbing, his legs stiff from— God, she was such a bleeding heart.

Or maybe she was just looking for excuses to invite him into her room.

Marley sighed in the darkness. Why couldn't she just stay angry with him? She shouldn't want him around. After Patrick's betrayal, she'd banished her former fiancé from her heart and mind. Had had zero desire ever to see his sorry face again. So why wasn't it that way with Caleb?

She lay in bed for eighteen more minutes, watching the red numbers on her alarm clock roll over. Finally, she couldn't stand it anymore.

Groaning, she pushed away the comforter and got up, bare feet padding toward the door. She threw it open, and sure enough, Caleb sat on the floor, his head resting against the door of the guest room.

"Get in here already," she mumbled.

He shifted, one hand on the gun holstered at his hip, the other behind his head as a makeshift pillow. "I'm fine out here."

She set her jaw. "Seriously, come in. I can't sleep knowing you're spending the night on the floor."

"I—"

She held up her hand to silence him. "Stop arguing," she mimicked, "and come in."

Looking extremely reluctant, Caleb stood up and followed her into the bedroom. He eyed the bed, and she noticed his throat working as he swallowed. She knew exactly what he was thinking. She was thinking it, too, and her body grew hot as she remembered everything they'd done on this bed only last night.

A wave of longing hit her as she thought about Caleb's hands touching her skin, the seductive swirl of his tongue, the strength of his body as he drove into her, over and over.

"Now what?" he asked with a sigh, turning to her for his next orders.

She hesitated. "We'll share the bed. It's big enough for both of us."

"Marley...this isn't a good idea."

"I don't care. It's one o'clock in the morning, I'm

exhausted, and I can't sleep knowing you're sitting on the hard floor." She marched to the bed and got under the covers, then shot him a pointed look.

Caleb seemed ready to protest again, but finally he just nodded, a resigned light in his eyes. Slowly, he removed his gun and holster and carefully placed them on the top of her dresser. Then he glanced down at his clothing, as if trying to figure out what the heck to do.

Marley averted her eyes as he reached for his zipper. She heard the soft rustle of his clothing falling to the floor and then he was lowering his big body onto her bed. The mattress sagged from the weight of him. Her pulse sped up.

He didn't get under the covers, just lay on top of them, flat on his back with his arms pressed to his sides. She was on her back, too, suddenly feeling nervous and slightly upset with herself. Her fingers tingled with the need to touch him. From the corner of her eye, she saw his bare chest rising and falling with each breath he took. And his masculine scent wrapped around her, spicy and musky and totally intoxicating.

She curled her fingers into fists to keep from reaching over and touching him. Staying completely still, she closed her eyes and tried to sleep, but her mind refused to shut off. She suddenly remembered something, and rolled onto her side to look at him. "What did you say to Hernandez in the hall?" she asked.

"Nothing important."

"It seemed important," she said. "And when he came back to question me, he was actually being kind of… nice. So either hell froze over or you got him to change his mind about me."

Caleb went quiet for a moment. "I reminded him that you're not Amanda James."

She wrinkled her forehead. "Who?"

"AJ got me a copy of Hernandez's file, which included the last case he worked." Caleb paused. "I probably shouldn't be telling you this."

"Don't you think I deserve to know why he's treated me so badly?"

He paused for a second beat, finally letting out a breath. "Amanda James was the girlfriend of a guy Hernandez was trying to pin a series of bank robberies on. She insisted she had no idea what her boyfriend was doing, that she played no part in the robberies, and she was inconsolable when Hernandez brought her in for questioning. She was just a kid, barely nineteen, and Hernandez felt protective of her."

Marley propped herself up on her elbow. "What happened?"

"The boyfriend was arrested but the judge let him out on bail. The day he got out, he and the girl robbed a grocery store, trying to get money to skip town. They ended up killing three people, including a ten-year-old kid."

Marley sucked in a breath. "Oh, God, that's awful."

"Yeah, it was," he agreed. "It turned out James knew about the robberies all along, she'd even participated in some, and Hernandez looked like a total fool."

Despite herself, she felt a pang of sympathy. "And then Patrick and I came along, and the Bonnie and Clyde thing was happening all over again."

"He didn't want to make another mistake, but he took it to the other extreme. Too lenient on the first suspect, too harsh on the second."

"I still don't like him," she said. "I get now why he was so hard on me, but I'm not sure that's a good enough reason to totally railroad someone."

"I agree."

They fell silent, and she lay there watching the rise of his chest, the way he stared directly at the ceiling as if he couldn't bear to look at her.

"Was it honestly real?" she whispered.

That got his attention. Very slowly, he turned to face her, looking into her eyes. "It was real," he murmured. "I lied about my job, but I didn't lie about who I am."

"And who are you, Caleb?"

"I'm…I'm just a man. I make mistakes. I obsess over the job sometimes. I've never been in a serious relationship, probably because I'm used to being alone. I've always been alone."

Each word sent an ache to her heart, until it squeezed so tight in her chest she could barely draw a breath. His voice was heavy with emotion, his face showing vulnerability she knew he hated to reveal.

"But not with you," he said, so quietly she had to lean forward to hear him. "I don't feel alone when I'm with you."

She couldn't help herself—she moved closer to him. Their faces were mere inches apart. Alarm bells rang in her head, warning her to stop this insanity before she fell into the same damn trap as before.

"It was real," he said again, his breath warm against her face. "More real than anything else in my life, sweetheart. All these years I've gone through the motions, done my job and made conversation with my coworkers. I pretended to be normal, all the while knowing I wasn't quite whole."

She shivered as he lifted his hand to touch her cheek, tenderly caressing her skin. "I wasn't pretending with you," he finished. "I lied, but I didn't pretend."

God, what was she supposed to do, to say? This was

the most open he'd ever been with her. His gruffness and cool composure was stripped away, leaving him bare and raw and *honest*.

Was she an idiot for wanting so badly to believe in that honesty?

Sensing where her thoughts had gone, Caleb's voice became desperate. "I'm not lying to you, Marley. It might be better if I was, because then I wouldn't have to feel…whatever it is I feel for you. It scares me. *You* scare me."

Her breath hitched as he slid closer, so that their bodies were touching. She felt his heartbeat vibrating against her breasts, which grew heavy with need. His eyes dropped to her mouth, and her surroundings faded as Caleb kissed her.

She couldn't pull back, couldn't push him away. Goosebumps rose on her bare arms, which twined around him. Her fingers touched the soft hair at the nape of his neck.

"We shouldn't… I shouldn't…" Her words got lost in the kiss, swept away as he teased her lips with his tongue then slipped it into her mouth, where she met each greedy thrust, swirling and exploring until they were both breathless.

"Can't you feel it?" he rasped against her trembling lips. "It feels right, Marley."

She wanted to disagree, but the objection refused to leave her mouth. She didn't want him to be right. She didn't want *this* to be right. But she couldn't stop kissing him, couldn't stop the need that rose inside her like a tidal wave.

She reached between them and slid her hand under the elastic waistband of his boxers. She grasped his erection, stroking it as he let out a husky groan. She couldn't fight the crazy urge to touch him. He nuzzled her neck, his mouth latching onto the soft flesh there.

A slow-burning fire spread through her body, pulsing between her legs and making her breasts tingle. When Caleb groaned against her throat and moved his hips to meet her hurried strokes, the fire burned even hotter.

"I need you inside me," she whispered.

Both his hands suddenly cupped her chin. He searched her face, looking hopeful and anxious and unbelievably aroused. "Are you sure?"

She nodded, shifting onto her back and parting her thighs. God, this was insane. She should hate this man, not want him. Kick him out, not pull him close. But the fire inside her refused to cool. Every nerve ending she possessed crackled with urgent need.

Caleb leaned over her and yanked open the drawer on the nightstand, rummaging around for the condoms they'd stashed there. He had his boxers off and a condom on before she could blink, and then he peeled her tiny boxer shorts and tank top off her body. He tossed them aside, along with her panties, and covered her body with his. With a slow and delicious thrust, he was inside her, eliciting simultaneous groans from each of their throats.

Pleasure gathered in her belly, intensifying as Caleb began to move. There was nothing rushed about his thrusts. He slid in and out, out and in, an indolent rhythm that made her whimper.

His warm hands stroked her face, his lips peppering kisses on her jaw, her neck, her shoulder.

"This is real," he murmured. "It's real, sweetheart."

His pace remained lazy, and not even the restless

lift of her hips deterred him. He made long, slow love to her, and when she looked up at his gorgeous face, the emotion she saw took her breath away.

Real. Yes, this felt real. She wrapped her arms around him and dragged her fingernails up and down the hard muscles of his back. The gentle tempo he'd set wasn't enough anymore. She wanted more. Needed more. With a little moan, she urged him to go faster, arching her back to take him deeper. When he still didn't comply, she raked her nails down his back and resorted to begging. "Please, Caleb...*please.*"

Whatever restraint he'd been holding onto snapped like a bungee cord, and then he was driving into her like a man possessed. "Christ," he choked out. "You're... I..."

He gave up on talking and kept moving, plunging into her until she could no longer bear it, until all her muscles tensed and...oh, *yes*. All thoughts drained out of her head as her body fragmented in sweet release. Flashes of light blinded her, while bursts of ecstasy went off in her body. She felt Caleb let go and she held him as he shook from release.

When the waves of her orgasm finally ebbed, common sense returned, urging Marley to push him away. She'd experienced a momentary relapse, a foolish lack of self-control, but now was the time to come back to reality. Caleb had lied to her, he'd hurt her, and even though she'd trusted him with her body just now, could she really trust him with her heart?

Yet her arms refused to let go of him, her legs refused to unhook from their perch on his trim hips. And her heart...her heart implored her to hold him even tighter.

So she did.

CALEB HAD NEVER BEEN ONE to question good fortune. Even that one Christmas when his current foster mom presented him with a brand-new baseball glove, he'd forced himself not to ask, "Why?" In his experience, people didn't give gifts without expecting something in return, but Marley…she'd given him something so incredibly important last night. He wasn't about to ruin that by spitting out all the questions biting at his tongue.

Do you forgive me?

Can you ever trust me again?

He couldn't help but remember the day in Marley's kitchen, when she'd asked him if he'd ever been in love and had looked so astounded when he'd admitted he hadn't. He might have a different answer now, if the unfamiliar warmth flowing through his veins was what he thought it was. It was funny—the women he'd dated in the past had wanted so badly for him to love them, but how could he, when he wasn't even sure what love felt like?

Now, he thought he might have an idea. The lump of tenderness that lodged in his throat whenever he looked into Marley's eyes. The heat that unfurled in his body whenever he touched her. The protective rush that shot through him when he thought about the danger she was in.

Was that love?

Sitting up in bed, Caleb watched as Marley moved around the bedroom, folding clothes, shoving a pair of shoes into the closet. She'd barely said two words since they woke up, and he was beginning to grow uneasy. Any second now, he expected her to tell him last night was a mistake and throw him out.

But she didn't do that. Rather, she strode to the

bathroom, then hesitated in the doorway and glanced over her shoulder. "Want to take a shower?"

He was off the bed and moving toward her in a nano-second.

Taking off the T-shirt she'd slipped into before they'd gone to sleep, she stepped into the shower stall. Caleb shucked his boxers and followed her in, wrapping his arms around her from behind as she turned on the faucet. Hot water poured out of the showerhead and Marley tilted her head, letting the water soak her honey-blond hair. She took a step back, giving him a turn under the spray while she reached for a poufy-looking thing and squirted a generous amount of body wash onto it. The scent of strawberries filled the small space. It smelled like Marley, sweet and feminine and unbelievably sexy.

He couldn't take his eyes off her as she washed herself, white suds sliding down her body and gathering in the valley of her breasts. She was so freaking gorgeous, creamy white skin, gentle curves and full breasts tipped with tight pink nipples.

He opened his mouth to say something. Tell her she was beautiful. Ask her if she needed help. But what came out was, "What does this mean?"

Handing him the pouf, she moved under the spray and let the water wash away the suds. For a long time, she didn't answer, and he just stood there, feeling slightly awkward as he dragged the fluffy sponge across his body, branding that strawberry scent into his own skin.

When she finally spoke, her voice came out in a sigh. "I don't know what it means."

Do you want me to stay?

He didn't utter the words, fearful of how she might respond. Instead, he asked the question to himself.

Did he want to stay?

His entire adult life had revolved around his job. He worked out of the New York office, but his assignments took him all over the country. Staying with Marley would mean not being able to take certain assignments, or maybe even leaving the agency altogether. It would be too hard, living apart for long periods at a time.

It astounded him that he could even consider any of this. His work was all he'd ever cared about. Previously, the notion of not having his job had brought a knot of panic to his gut.

Now, that panic arose when he imagined leaving Marley. He wanted to stay here with her. To help her renovate her house and go to Sunday barbecues at her dad's place. To make love to her every night and wake up next to her every morning.

"We shouldn't talk about it right now." Marley's soft voice pulled him out of his disconcerting thoughts. "I don't have the energy for it. I just want Patrick to be caught."

Sliding open the steamed-up door, Marley got out of the shower, her body slick and rosy pink. Caleb quickly rinsed, then turned off the faucet. He was just getting out when Marley let out a squeak followed by an irritated curse.

"You okay?" he asked.

She hopped on one foot, holding the other one with a wet hand and rubbing her big toe. "Yeah, I'm fine. I just stubbed my toe on that loose tile again."

He looked at the floor. One of the tiles had popped out of place, thanks to Marley's foot.

"I definitely need to retile," she grumbled, moving

to the door and swiping a terry-cloth robe from the hook there.

Caleb continued to stare at the tile. Why had a tile in the middle of the floor come loose? Something wasn't right. "I think…" Getting out of the shower, he bent down to the floor, dripping water all over the place. "There's something here."

He lifted the tile, squinting into the space beneath. Instead of the plywood that should have been there, someone had sawed out a jagged square, revealing the cavity beneath the sub-floor. A dark little hiding place. Slowly, Caleb stuck his hand in, feeling around until his fingers made contact with plastic. He gripped what felt like an envelope, using only his thumb and forefinger to pull it out.

"What is that?" Marley asked.

Caleb studied the envelope, which was enclosed in a clear plastic bag. It felt bulky, and when he gingerly removed it from the bag and lifted the flap, his breath caught in his throat.

Marley stepped closer, peering down at the envelope in his hands. She gasped. "Is that…money?"

He stared at the thick stacks of bills, four of them individually wrapped with elastic bands. All hundreds, and each stack had to contain at least fifty grand.

Dropping the flap, Caleb tucked the envelope back in the bag and stood up. "Well, I think we know why Patrick's still in town," he remarked with a sigh.

14

MARLEY STOOD IN FRONT of the sliding door leading to her backyard and stared at the sparrows pecking at the seeds in her bird feeder. Male voices drifted in from the living room—Caleb was in there with Jamison and D'Amato, the two DEA agents who'd been posted outside during the night. They were discussing the money Caleb had discovered in the bathroom, and she preferred not to be there for that.

She still couldn't believe it. Patrick had stashed two hundred thousand dollars under her floor. She'd probably walked over that spot hundreds of times in the past few months, completely oblivious to what lay below. The thought that her bathroom floor had been housing Patrick's drug money for so long made her want to cry.

Caleb was certain Patrick would come back for the money. It was probably the only reason he hadn't fled the city earlier. He had to know by now that their bank account had been frozen. Caleb told her that the bank wouldn't authorize any transfers *out* of the account.

Patrick must be pretty desperate by now, she thought,

her stomach churning. She grew even more uneasy when her cell phone vibrated in her purse, which sat on the kitchen counter. It was probably Gwen, or maybe her brother or her dad, whose calls she'd been avoiding since last night. Her best friend and family had no idea what had happened yesterday—finding Lydia White tied up in her bedroom, discovering Patrick's drug money.

She hadn't called because she didn't want to scare them any further. Patrick's stunt at the hospital already had everyone on edge.

She fished the phone out of her bag, sighing when she saw her dad's number flashing on the screen. This was his third call in the past hour. If she continued to not pick up, he and Sam would probably drive over in a panic. That was one scene she wouldn't mind avoiding.

"Hey, Dad," she said as she pressed the talk button.

"Hey, sweet pea."

Shock slammed into her like a baseball bat, sucking the oxygen right out of her lungs.

"Don't say my name," Patrick added swiftly. "Are you alone?"

Her fingers shook against the phone. "Y-yes."

"Good. If anyone comes in, you're talking to your father."

She choked down the hard lump of terror obstructing her throat. "Why are you calling from this number?"

"Because I'm having a nice little visit with your father," Patrick answered in a pleasant voice. "Sammy's here, too, but I'm afraid I had to knock him out. He was being very difficult."

A chill rushed over her. "Don't you dare hurt either one of them."

"I'm not going to hurt anyone." He sounded annoyed. "Your father's sitting right here beside me, not a hair on his head disturbed."

"Let me talk to him," she blurted. Her heart hammered in her chest, so fast she feared it might stop beating altogether. "I want to talk to him."

"Fine, but be quick. You and I have some things to discuss."

There was a shuffling noise, and then, to her sheer relief, her father came on the line. "Sweetheart?"

"Daddy?" she whispered. "Oh, God, Dad, are you okay?"

"I'm all right," her father replied, but the slight quiver in his voice told her he was anything but all right.

"Has he hurt you?"

"No." *Not yet,* was what he seemed to be saying. Her dad grew urgent, his words coming out so fast she struggled to keep up. "Don't do a thing he asks, Marley. Your brother and I will be okay. Whatever he wants, don't give it to him. Do you hear me, sweetheart, don't—"

An angry curse whipped through the extension, and then Patrick returned. "Your father's trying to be a hero," he said with a chuckle. "But we both know you're not going to leave him at my mercy, right, *sweet pea?*"

"What do you want?"

"I need you to bring me something. There's some money stashed in your house. It's hidden under…"

Marley tuned him out, the sound of footsteps sending alarm spinning through her. She heard the front door shut, then more footsteps coming toward the kitchen. Caleb appeared in the doorway a second later, and she quickly held up her hand to silence him.

His blue eyes immediately hardened as he looked at the cell phone pressed up to her ear.

"—and bring it to your father's house," Patrick finished. "One hour, Marley."

An unsteady breath squeezed out of her lungs. "I c-can't. They're watching me."

"The cops?"

"Yeah. They're next door. And one is upstairs right now," she said, avoiding Caleb's eyes. "I can't leave without them knowing."

"You're a smart girl. I'm sure you'll find a way." Patrick's voice turned to ice. "You sure found a way to screw someone else while I was gone."

She swallowed. "I…"

"I don't want to hear your excuses," Patrick snapped. "Get the money and bring it to me, or you can say goodbye to your baby brother and your daddy."

"Please, don't hurt—"

"And you'd better be alone," he interrupted. "I'll be watching you pull up, and if I sense anything funny, your father and junior die."

He hung up, and Marley sagged against the counter. She gasped for air, salty tears welling up and coating her eyelashes. A pair of warm arms surrounded her, steadying her before she could keel over.

She whirled around and pressed her face against Caleb's strong chest, her tears soaking the front of his shirt. "He has my dad and brother," she wheezed between sobs. "He's going to kill them if I don't bring him the money."

Caleb's hands stroked her back, soothing her, bringing warmth to her suddenly freezing body. He tangled his fingers in her hair and angled her head so she was looking up at him. "It's okay," he murmured. "It'll be okay."

"How can you say that? He's going to kill them!"

"I won't let him," Caleb replied. He used his thumb to wipe away her tears. "I won't let him hurt them, Marley."

"What are we going to do? He wants me to bring the money in an hour, and I have to go alone. If I bring the cops, he said he'll kill them."

Whatever confidence she lacked at the moment, Caleb made up for in spades. He released her and picked up the radio he'd put on the counter, alerting AJ and the others to the situation. As she stood there, shaken up and afraid, he placed a call to Hernandez and then to a man he referred to as Stevens.

Fifteen minutes later, Caleb had efficiently assembled a team in her living room, except for Stevens, who listened in on speakerphone.

Marley could barely focus as the men discussed the situation in urgent tones. Patrick had her father and Sam. He'd taken so much from her already. Several pieces of her heart, her ability to trust, her confidence and now he wanted to take her family?

"We can use a decoy," she heard Hernandez suggest.

Marley's head whipped up.

"We've got an officer in vice who's about Marley's height and build," the detective continued. "We'll set her up with a wig and a wire, and send her in to—"

"No."

The men swiveled their heads in her direction, stunned into silence by the vehemence in that one word.

"Marley," Caleb began, "I know you're upset, but

we're doing everything we can to get your dad and brother back."

"You can't send in a decoy," she insisted. "He'll know."

Hernandez glanced at her in annoyance. "Officer Gray is trained to—"

"I don't give a damn what she's trained to do," she snapped. "I'm telling you, Patrick will know the second she gets out of the car that she isn't me. We were engaged, Detective. He'll *know*."

Silence descended over the room again.

"What exactly are you getting at?" Caleb asked, sounding extremely wary.

She drew in a steadying breath. "I should be the one to go."

"No way," Caleb jumped to his feet. "No way, Marley."

"Why not? I can take the money, give it to him in exchange for my dad and Sammy, and then you guys can catch him when he tries to leave."

"It's not that simple," Caleb said. "He's bound to have a weapon. He could shoot you and your family the second he gets the cash."

She lifted her chin. "So give me a bulletproof vest."

"And if he shoots you in the head?"

She swallowed hard. "I need to do this, Caleb. I won't let him hurt my family, and if you try to send in some fake version of me, he *will* hurt them."

She studied the faces of the men. Caleb's partner was looking at her with what appeared to be admiration, the two DEA agents looked as if they were mulling over what she'd said, the SDPD officers were stone-faced and Hernandez watched her with serious dark eyes.

"Do you think you can get him outside?" the detective asked.

Caleb spun around to glare at Hernandez. "What are you doing? She's not going in there, damn it!"

"It could work," Hernandez replied. "She gives him the money, and then convinces him she wants to run off with him. Kincaid Sr. and Jr. remain in the house, and Marley and Grier head outside where we'll have a team waiting."

"He'll spot us," AJ spoke up.

"Not if we stay out of sight until Marley gives the signal they're coming out," Hernandez countered. He looked over at her again. "Do you think you'll be able to do this?"

She hesitated. Convince Patrick she still loved him, that she wanted to flee the country with him? The very idea of seeing his face again made her feel sick.

But what about her dad? What about Sammy? Could she really let them be taken away from her simply because she felt ill at the thought of being near Patrick?

She exhaled. "I can do it."

"No," Caleb said again. He stepped toward her, his features hard. "I won't let you put your life in danger. We can handle this."

"No, you can't. Patrick won't open that door to anyone but me."

She stared into Caleb's blue eyes, floored by the agony she saw in them. He was scared. Scared for her.

"I'm scared, too," she murmured as if he'd vocalized his fear. "But you'll be right outside to protect me."

He nodded. "Always," he said softly.

Something inside her chest dislodged. It took her a moment to figure out what it was—the jagged little pieces of anger and bitterness that had clung to her heart after Caleb had told her the truth. The shards had disappeared, as an important realization dawned on her. This man would do anything to protect her. She mattered to him.

Acceptance settled over her like a warm blanket. Caleb wasn't a sick voyeur who'd decided to prey on her. He was a cop on a stakeout, a man trying to avenge his friend's death. Could she really hold that against him? He might have lied to her, but now he was doing everything in his power to keep her safe.

"I can do this, Caleb," she said, her voice barely a whisper. "Trust me to do this."

His shoulders tightened at the word *trust*. She knew what he was thinking. The question he'd been wanting to ask her since last night. *Can you trust me again?*

Now she was asking it of him.

And even though she could tell it went against everything he believed in, letting someone else venture into a dangerous situation instead of him, he nodded and said, "I trust you."

MARLEY'S ENTIRE BODY trembled as she shut off the engine of her convertible. The bungalow she'd grown up in, where her dad and brother still lived, looked so harmless and cozy, but there was nothing harmless about this situation, was there? Patrick was inside that house, holding her family hostage, all so he could get his greedy hands on some cash. To flee from the law, to get away with murder.

"I really hope you can hear this," she muttered.

She didn't look down at her chest, in case Patrick was watching her from the window, but the transmitter taped inside her bra dug into her skin, reminding her of the danger she was about to walk into.

Caleb's partner assured her that every word would be recorded and transmitted to the team's earpieces in real time. They would know what was going on every second she was in the house. If she said the panic word, agents would storm the house in less than a minute. If she convinced Patrick she wanted to leave town with him, she would say the go word and the arrest would be made after Caleb gave her the signal to wrench away from Patrick's side.

Taking a breath, she picked up her purse, which contained the two hundred thousand dollars. The agents had opted not to tag the money with dye, instead tucking a tiny GPS transmitter into one of the stacks, in case Patrick managed another great escape.

She slung her purse over her shoulder and got out of the car. Her legs shook as she stepped onto the gravel driveway. She took a few more seconds to breathe, to gather her composure, and then she walked up the path to the front door.

Her hand wavered as she knocked on the door. It opened instantly, and for the first time in three months, Marley laid eyes on the man she'd been engaged to marry.

He looked exactly the same. Brown hair cut in a neat, no-nonsense style, wiry body covered with a pair of khakis and a polo shirt. Only his brown eyes looked different. Wilder. Colder.

Patrick looked pleased as he peered past her shoulders and examined the deserted street. He also seemed completely unruffled by the fact that he was pointing a gun at her.

"You came alone. Good girl."

She yelped as he grabbed her arm and hauled her into the house, closing and locking the door behind them.

"Where's my dad and brother?" she demanded.

He ignored the question. "Did you bring the money?"

She nodded.

"Give it to me."

She reached into her purse, pulled out the envelope, and handed it to him. Keeping his gun trained on her, he stuck a hand into the bag and took out the envelope. Opening the flap, he flipped through the thick stacks of bills.

Marley held her breath, praying he wouldn't stumble across the transmitter. It was smaller than a watch battery, hard to find unless he diligently examined each bill, which he didn't.

She exhaled slowly. "It's all there."

"I can see that," he replied.

"Can I see my family now?"

"You don't get to ask me questions." He leaned closer and jammed the barrel of the gun into her side.

She stared up at him, shocked by the emptiness she saw in his eyes. How could this be the same man she'd fallen in love with? The last time she'd seen Patrick, he'd been playful and loving as he kissed her goodbye and left for a web-design convention that would last all weekend.

There had never been a convention, only an illegal gathering to distribute drugs.

He looked like a total stranger now. Those empty eyes. The effortless way he gripped the gun, as if holding someone at gunpoint was no biggie to him.

Marley blinked back tears. She pressed her lips together, forcing herself not to plead with him. She was anxious to make sure her dad and Sam were alive, but she didn't want to push him.

Patrick's hard gaze connected with hers, and the unrestrained anger on his face made her apprehensive. She suspected he might snap at any second, just go ahead and shoot her, but to her surprise, his features crumpled with anguish. "How could you cheat on me?" he asked.

This was it. Her chance to diffuse the situation.

"You slept with that cop," Patrick continued, bitterness drenching each word. "You couldn't wait three damn months?"

She tried to speak, but he cut her off, his expression suddenly wistful. "You know, I came back here for you, Marley."

She feigned surprise. "You did?"

"Yeah." A faraway note entered his voice. "I had it all planned. We'd head for South America, buy a little house on the beach, spend the rest of our lives lying on the sand, just the two of us."

Marley was tempted to point out how delusional that sounded—he was a fugitive, for Pete's sake—but she stayed quiet. She couldn't blow this. She'd promised Caleb she could handle this, and antagonizing Patrick was not the way to do it.

"That sounds wonderful," she said, smiling up at him.

"Then why couldn't you wait for me?" he spat out. "Instead of having faith that I'd come for you, you went out and screwed the first guy you saw."

She took a deep breath. "I did it for you."

Patrick's entire body stiffened. "What did you say?"

"I said I did it for you," she whispered.

Patrick didn't speak, but she could swear the pressure of his gun eased up. His dark eyes searched her face. For what seemed like hours. She grew uncomfortable, scared, panicked, under that intense scrutiny. When she couldn't stand it anymore, she said, "Why are you looking at me?"

"I'm trying to figure out if you're telling me the truth."

Her heart raced. "I am."

"How?" he asked. "How was that for me, you banging another guy?"

She edged closer to him, flinching when the gun dug into her side again. "I missed you so much," she confessed. "I was so worried, Patrick. I didn't know where you were, if you were okay... And then this cop showed up, pretending to be my neighbor. I knew right away what he was up to."

"You did?"

"Of course. I would never go to bed with another man unless I had a good reason. You know that."

He looked deep into her eyes, a hesitant smile lifting one corner of his mouth. "You got close to him to get information? To protect me?"

"I got close to him so he wouldn't get close to finding *you*," she replied. "I had to be sure he wasn't making headway locating you."

Patrick hesitated, then released a sigh. "I would have done the same thing, babe."

"Really?" She gave him a pleading look. "Do you forgive me, Patrick? I was only trying to help."

He lowered the gun and slid closer to her, stroking her cheek with his cold fingers. "Of course I forgive you. I love you, Marley. I've been thinking of nothing but you the last three months."

"Why didn't you tell me the truth? You know I would have stood by you, no matter what you did for a living."

He lowered his eyes and shrugged. "I know. I'm sorry. I should have trusted you."

"Yes," she agreed in a petulant voice.

"Well, I trust you now." He gently tucked a strand of hair behind her ear. "And I promise I'll spend the rest of my life making this up to you."

He stuck the gun in the waistband of his jeans, every last iota of rage and resentment draining from his face, replaced with pure, delusional joy. Oh, God, he was insane. He seriously believed she was telling the truth. That she'd gotten close to Caleb to find out what the cops were doing.

So she could protect Patrick.

Choking back her disbelief, she said, "Can I really go with you?"

He gave her a warm smile, reminding her of the day she'd met him in the hospital, how charming he'd been. "I want you by my side, sweet pea, and I always will." He wavered for a moment. "What about your dad? And Sam? Can you leave them? I know how much your family means to you."

Then why are you holding them hostage? she wanted to scream.

Her nerves began to unravel like an old sweater, and she had to force herself to stay in character. "You mean more," she said simply.

His entire face lit up, and all of a sudden he was the man she'd been going to marry. Preppy, handsome, easygoing smile.

"We should go then," he said, urgency lining his tone. "How did you get away from the cops?"

She fed him the story she and Caleb had concocted. "I insisted I wanted to go into work. An agent followed me to the hospital, and then I switched clothes with Gwen and snuck out."

Patrick sounded surprised. "Gwen helped you?"

"Of course." Marley smiled. "She knows how much I still love you."

"God, sweet pea, I missed you so much," Patrick burst out, taking a step toward her.

His gaze dropped to her mouth and something in his expression shifted. To her dismay, she saw a spark of lust there. Horror gripped her insides as he dipped his head. He was going to kiss her.

There was no way she would be able to kiss him back. The very thought of placing her lips on his repulsed her.

Faking a smile, she pressed her index finger to his mouth and laughed. "Hold that thought. We need to go, remember?" She put on a concerned look. "But first I want to make sure Dad and Sam are okay, and say goodbye to them. Is that okay?"

The reverent expression on his face told he would give her the moon if she asked.

"Okay, you can say your goodbyes," he conceded. "Let's get this show on the road before I go crazy with impatience. I want to start our life together, Marley."

She looked him square in the eye and said, "Me, too."

15

CALEB CROUCHED BEHIND the tall hedges of the house three doors down from the Kincaid bungalow. Fear continued to slither up and down his spine like a hungry snake, cold and relentless. He'd been in this state since the moment he'd agreed to let Marley go and meet Patrick.

For the last ten minutes, he'd been listening to their conversation on his earpiece while AJ and Hernandez coordinated with the other agents and police officers on the scene. Four teams had been set up—all out of Patrick's line of sight—and they were all raring to go. Waiting for Marley to say the word.

"She's good," Hernandez admitted with great reluctance as he came up beside Caleb.

Marley had just convinced Grier she was willing to leave her family for him. To anyone else, her tone must sound strong and confident. Ringing with conviction.

But Caleb had spent enough time with her to recognize the nuances of her voice. He knew when she was fighting back laughter, when she was aroused, when she felt vulnerable.

And when she was scared out of her wits, the way she was right now.

"She's terrified," he corrected.

Hernandez's shoulders drooped. "I know." He sounded ashamed as he added, "And I know you despise me for the way I treated her."

Caleb sighed. "I already told you, I understand what drove you to it. The James case hit you hard, I get that."

The detective gave a sad nod. "Yeah, it did." He glanced at the four men standing nearby. They were armed and ready to take down the bastard whose clutches Marley had willingly put herself in. "But I'm not sure that excuses the way I acted."

Caleb didn't answer, too distracted by the relieved cry that rang in his ear. Patrick had just taken Marley to her father, who Caleb figured was tied up as he heard Marley ask about his wrists. Sam Sr. was apparently in perfect health, unlike his son. "Did you have to knock him unconscious?" Marley asked.

"He tried to attack me," came Patrick's muffled voice. "It's only a sedative, sweet pea. He'll come to in an hour or so."

As Caleb listened, Marley tried to convince Patrick to untie her father, but he wouldn't have it, insisting that her brother would take care of the bindings when he woke up. Now that Marley had seen to her family's safety, Patrick was all action, going on about the money and the new IDs he'd arranged for them.

Footsteps echoed in Caleb's ears. His muscles tensed. They were heading for the door.

"I'm so happy we're doing this," Marley said, sounding nearly giddy. "I've always wanted to go to South America." She giggled. "The most exciting place I've ever been to is Disneyland."

Disneyland—there it was, the go word.

Caleb and his team sprung into action.

"Let's move," Hernandez hissed.

The men emerged from their hiding place, moving in unison toward the Kincaid bungalow. They reached the front lawn just as Patrick and Marley stepped outside.

Grier's eyes flashed with red-hot fury at the sight of Caleb and the other men. He spun around as two cruisers, along with an unmarked SUV, flew into sight. One cruiser drove directly onto the front lawn, another came to a grinding halt in the driveway, while the third skidded over the curb. Car doors opened and slammed, men in tactical gear, carrying gleaming black weapons, swarmed the yard.

Caleb heard his own voice shout, "Hands in the air, Grier!"

Rather than obey, Grier's right hand snapped down to his waist and he whipped out a gun. Caleb's heart dropped to the pit of his stomach as Grier then took that gun and jammed it into Marley's temple.

"I'll shoot her!" Grier screamed, his face bright crimson.

"Put the gun down," Caleb ordered. He took another step forward.

"Don't move!" Patrick yelled.

Caleb stopped in his tracks and shot a sideways look at Agent Tony D'Amato, who was kneeling behind the open door of the police cruiser on the lawn. D'Amato lifted his rifle slightly, asking a silent question, which Caleb answered with a hard glare. D'Amato wanted to take out Grier. Caleb wanted the same thing. But there was no way in hell he was doing anything until Marley was out of the line of fire.

He forced himself not to look at her, but it was damn near impossible. Her heart-shaped face was ashen. She stood motionless, with Grier's weapon pressed to her temple.

"You're completely surrounded," Caleb told Grier. He lowered his voice. "Just let her go and give yourself up, Patrick. This doesn't have to end with another life on your hands."

"I killed that agent in self-defense! I'm not a murderer!"

"Of course not," Caleb soothed. He took another step. "But you will be, if you use that gun on Marley."

"Don't say her name," Grier hissed. "She doesn't belong to you. She belongs to me!"

Another step. "Then I'm sure you don't want to hurt her, Patrick. I know you care about her."

Grier's features twisted. "She's mine." He jabbed the gun into Marley's temple again. "But I will kill her if you sons of bitches don't get out of my way. Marley and I have a plane to catch."

Caleb moved closer, then stopped and caught Marley's eye. The panic on her face tore at his insides, but he pushed away the primal urge to launch himself at Patrick Grier and wrench Marley away from him. Instead, he sent her the signal they'd agreed on back at her house, two quick nods and the lift of his right shoulder.

She answered with an imperceptible nod and followed his orders to a T.

Pride mingled with the fear pumping through Caleb's blood as Marley made her move. With a little cry, she pretended to trip, then dove to the side, pressing her body flat to the ground.

While Patrick blinked with shock at losing his

hostage, Caleb charged forward. "Put the gun down!" he yelled.

Grier blinked again. He suddenly snapped out of whatever trance he'd gone into, his lips tightening. He stared at Caleb running toward him, then at Marley, who was a couple of yards to his left.

With lightning speed, he spun the gun at Marley.

Caleb didn't hesitate. He squeezed the trigger of his Glock, eliciting an outraged shriek of pain from Patrick as his arm took a hit. The other man stumbled, but not before his gun spat out a wild, desperate bullet in Marley's direction.

A bullet that Caleb dove in front of.

MARLEY LIFTED HERSELF onto her elbows in time to see Caleb's big, strong body thudding to the ground.

Chaos ensued. The hurried footsteps of the other agents rushing for Patrick. Patrick's shouts of indignation as he was thrown down, his arms yanked behind his back.

Still stunned, Marley watched as a pair of handcuffs were snapped around Patrick's wrists. And then the agents hauled him toward one of the cars, while he spat and struggled.

She winced when she heard him call her name.

"Marley!" he wailed. "You tricked me! You little bitch!"

He was still shouting at her as the cops shoved him into the cruiser.

"Are you okay?" a deep voice asked, and then a big hand helped her to her feet.

She flinched when she realized the hand belonged to Detective Miguel Hernandez. "I'm fine," she squeezed out.

"Ms. Kincaid," the detective started awkwardly. "I wanted to apologize for—"

She was already rushing away before he could finish the sentence. She didn't want or need Hernandez's apology, not when Caleb lay there on the grass after taking the bullet that was meant for her. What if the bullet had missed the vest?

"Caleb," she said urgently as she fell to her knees beside him.

He let out a groan and then, to her relief, sat up. Marley scanned his torso, wincing at the neat hole in the middle of his dark-blue button-down shirt.

"It got the vest, right?" She ran her fingers over him, checking for damage.

With a soft chuckle, he unbuttoned his shirt and spread it apart, revealing the black Kevlar vest molded to his broad chest. A small bullet was lodged in the material, an inch to the right of Caleb's heart.

"They always aim for the vest," he said gruffly.

"Unless they're aiming at your head," she said, mimicking his earlier words. "Seriously, are you okay?"

"I feel like I got the wind knocked out of me, but I'm okay. I'm more worried about you." Caleb stumbled to his feet, pulling her up with him. "Did he hurt you?"

She stared into his gorgeous blue eyes and the love and concern she saw shining there robbed her of breath. He was worried about *her*. He'd just taken a bullet while trying to save her, and he was thinking about her?

"He didn't hurt me," she assured him. "He was too busy planning our happy little life together. I did good, didn't I? I really had him going."

Caleb's eyes became cloudy. "You took a big risk, Marley. You could have gotten yourself killed."

"I knew you would protect me," she murmured. "I knew you would save me."

He opened his mouth to respond, but someone called his name. Agent D'Amato, a tall man with shaggy red hair, stalked toward them. "Agent Ford, we're taking the perp to lock-up. Stevens said you'd want to head up the interrogation."

Caleb didn't even glance at the other man. "You take care of it, D'Amato. I'm staying here."

"Yes, sir."

As the other agent walked toward the cruiser by the curb, Marley shot Caleb an inquiring look. "Shouldn't you go with them? You've been working this case for months. Don't you want to be there to see it come to a close?"

He shook his head. "I'm not leaving you. D'Amato and AJ can take care of Grier. I need to take care of you."

"I told you, I'm fine. I—" She halted. "But I do want to see Dad and Sam."

He reached out for her arm, stopping her. "Wait. I...I wanted to tell you something."

He bent forward a little, and she experienced a spark of concern, but when he met her eyes again, she realized the pain he was feeling had nothing to do with the fact that he'd been shot. "I thought he was going to kill you," Caleb whispered.

"But he didn't. I don't even have a scratch, Caleb. I promise you."

"I..." He released a breath with obvious effort. "I watched him hold that gun to your head, and I knew that...that if he pulled the trigger, I'd die right along with you."

Her heart did a little flip. "Caleb..."

"Please, I have to say this." He swallowed. "I know this isn't the time to ask for your forgiveness, or to figure out the future, but I need to say this."

Tears pricked at her eyelids. She tried to speak, but he pressed his fingers to her lips. "I love you," he said thickly.

All around them, things were still bustling. The cruisers were speeding away, sirens flashing. Several residents gathered on their front porches and lawns, whispering as they stared at the scene across the street. But Marley was oblivious to the activity. She couldn't look away from Caleb.

"I didn't think it could ever happen to me, I was always too shut off from people, but I fell in love with you." His voice cracked. "You made me see that there's more to life than just work. That I don't need to control my emotions all the time."

Marley was stunned. It was impossible to breathe, let alone speak.

At her lack of response, Caleb barreled on. "I'm sorry I lied to you. But I do love you, Marley, and I want to be with you."

She stood rooted in place, so overcome with joy she was unable to say a word.

Caleb's broad shoulders sagged. "Sorry, I guess this isn't the time to unload all this on you. I know you want to see your family." He let out a breath. "Okay, go do that. I guess I'll go to the station and we can talk later."

He started to walk away. His normally smooth strides were ungainly, as if walking in a straight line took too much effort.

She stood there, dumbfounded, then cleared her throat and shook her head, regaining her senses. "What the heck are you doing? Come back here," she called after him.

He froze, then looked over his shoulder, revealing his unbelievably gorgeous profile. Slowly, he turned to face her. A few yards separated them, but despite the distance, Marley could swear she heard his heart pounding.

"You're angry," he said with a sigh, bridging the distance between them.

She shot him a no-kidding look. "You were going to leave just like that?"

"You didn't say anything. I figured…you might need space or something."

The awkwardness of his voice made her laugh. God, he could be totally clueless sometimes. She thought of the way he'd launched himself in front of her when Patrick pulled the trigger. How he'd chosen to stay behind with her instead of going to the station to process the criminal he'd been hunting for months. He'd been so confident, so determined to protect her. And now he was standing here, back to his gruff, serious self, missing every last signal she sent in his direction.

"I didn't say anything because your words made me all emotional, you idiot."

The corner of his mouth lifted in a hopeful smile. "So you don't want me to go?"

"Of course I don't want you to go."

"Are you sure?" he asked, searching her face.

She nodded. Her throat went tight again, but she managed to say the most important thing. "I love you."

"You love me," he echoed in amazement.

"Yes." She drew in a breath and decided to do something crazy—trust him again. "I'm willing to work on the whole trust-and-forgiveness thing…if you're willing to stay."

Caleb touched her cheek so gently she felt like crying again, this time with joy. "I'm not going anywhere." He smiled ruefully. "Scratch that. I will need to go to Virginia to be debriefed about the case, but when I'm there, I'll request an immediate transfer to the west coast." He stroked her lips with his thumb. "And if they deny my request, I'll quit."

Her heart skipped a beat. "Are you serious?"

"You're more important to me than a job," he said.

Marley stood on her tiptoes and brushed her lips over his. Smiling, she pulled away. "I have one more condition for taking you back."

He grinned. "I knew this was too easy. Okay, lay it on me."

"You have to promise never to videotape me again."

A glimmer of guilt filled his eyes. He opened his mouth, but she raised her hand, adding, "At least *ask* me first, will you?"

The guilt faded into amusement. His smile consumed his entire face as he drew her into his arms and bent close to her ear. "There will never be another videotape of you again, sweetheart. Unless you want it." His voice grew husky as he murmured, "And if you do, let's make sure you're naked next time. I really like it when you're naked."

Laughing, Marley wrapped her arms around his neck and leaned in for one of Caleb's warm, toe-curling kisses. As their lips met, her heart sang with delight and forgiveness and trust.

And most importantly, love.

Epilogue

"SO WHAT DO YOU THINK?" Marley asked, holding up the two paint swatches so Caleb could give his opinion.

He frowned. "They're both green."

"Actually, this one is Serene Forest and this one is Leafy Splendor."

"They're *green*."

Marley sighed. Okay, it was official. When it came to paint advice, Caleb was terrible. From now on, she'd just ask her dad or brother for input.

"I'm picking Leafy Splendor," she said. "If you don't like it, tough."

Caleb looked beyond relieved. "You know, it amazes me that it took you this long to figure out I don't know anything about picking colors. Put a hammer or paintbrush in my hand and tell me what to do, and I'm fine, but colors? That's your job, sweetheart."

"I'm just trying to let you in on the decision-making process. That's what engaged couples do, you know." She held up her left hand and wiggled her ring finger.

The diamond engagement ring sparkled under the kitchen light.

Caleb's mouth curved in a crooked smile, not so rare these days. He always seemed to be smiling when they were together. "I still can't get enough of hearing that word. *Engaged.*"

The wonder in his eyes made her smile, too. She knew exactly what he meant. She couldn't stop looking down at the ring, just to make sure she hadn't imagined its presence.

The past eight months with Caleb had been the best of her life. She still couldn't believe all the changes he'd made for her. Leaving the DEA, taking the detective job with the San Diego Police Department. Ironically, his partner was none other than Miguel Hernandez, but Marley had begun warming up to the man who'd formerly treated her like a criminal. Hernandez had apologized numerous times for his behavior, though she'd barely thought about any of that for months now.

She'd have to think about it again soon, however. Patrick's trial started next month, and she'd been called as a witness. With all the charges her ex faced, she doubted her testimony even mattered. Murder, trafficking, attempted kidnapping, attempted murder. The prosecutor had assured Marley that Patrick would be in jail for the rest of his life, a notion that pleased her immensely.

But she didn't dwell on Patrick much anymore. What she and Caleb had was better than anything she could have imagined. Love, trust, laughter... Even her brother admitted the two of them made a scarily perfect match. It didn't hurt that Caleb had helped Sam and Marley's dad finish a huge construction job the other month. Nothing to kick-start some male bonding like renovating a house.

Caleb grabbed the Leafy Splendor paint swatch from the counter and sighed. "So, Color World?"

She was about to nod, but then she met his eyes, and the familiar expression on his face made her laugh.

"Don't give me the sex look," she said, wagging her finger. "One of these days you're just going to have to suck it up and buy some paint with me."

"One of these days," he agreed. He let the paint swatch drop from his hand and moved his fingers to her mouth, stroking her lips as his blue eyes smoldered with heat. "But today? No, I think we can find something more interesting to do."

She tilted her head. "Prove it."

With a grin, Caleb removed every scrap of clothing from her body.

And proved to her that there were, indeed, *much* more important things than paint.

* * * * *

COMING NEXT MONTH

Available September 27, 2011

#639 TOO WICKED TO KEEP
Legendary Lovers
Julie Leto

#640 DEVIL IN DRESS BLUES
Uniformly Hot!
Karen Foley

#641 THE MIGHTY QUINNS: RILEY
The Mighty Quinns
Kate Hoffmann

#642 NORTHERN FASCINATION
Alaskan Heat
Jennifer LaBrecque

#643 RIDING THE STORM
The Wrong Bed: Again and Again
Joanne Rock

#644 ROYALLY SEDUCED
A Real Prince
Marie Donovan

You can find more information on upcoming
Harlequin® titles, free excerpts and more at
www.HarlequinInsideRomance.com.

*Harlequin Romantic Suspense presents the latest book
in the scorching new* KELLEY LEGACY *miniseries
from best-loved veteran series author Carla Cassidy*

*Scandal is the name of the game as the Kelley family fights
to preserve their legacy, their hearts...and their lives.*

Read on for an excerpt from the fourth title
RANCHER UNDER COVER

*Available October 2011
from Harlequin Romantic Suspense*

"Would you like a drink?" Caitlin asked as she walked
to the minibar in the corner of the room. She felt as if she
needed to chug a beer or two for courage.

"No, thanks. I'm not much of a drinking man," he
replied.

She raised an eyebrow and looked at him curiously as she
poured herself a glass of wine. "A ranch hand who doesn't
enjoy a drink? I think maybe that's a first."

He smiled easily. "There was a six-month period in my
life when I drank too much. I pulled myself out of the bottom of a bottle a little over seven years ago and I've never
looked back."

"That's admirable, to know you have a problem and then
fix it."

Those broad shoulders of his moved up and down in
an easy shrug. "I don't know how admirable it was, all I
knew at the time was that I had a choice to make between
living and dying and I decided living was definitely more
appealing."

She wanted to ask him what had happened preceding
that six-month period that had plunged him into the bottom

of the bottle, but she didn't want to know too much about him. Personal information might produce a false sense of intimacy that she didn't need, didn't want in her life.

"Please, sit down," she said, and gestured him to the table. She had never felt so on edge, so awkward in her life.

"After you," he replied.

She was aware of his gaze intensely focused on her as she rounded the table and sat in the chair, and she wanted to tell him to stop looking at her as if she were a delectable dessert he intended to savor later.

Watch Caitlin and Rhett's sensual saga unfold amidst the shocking, ripped-from-the-headlines drama of the Kelley Legacy miniseries in

RANCHER UNDER COVER

Available October 2011 only from Harlequin Romantic Suspense, wherever books are sold.

Harlequin *Presents*®

USA TODAY bestselling author

Carol Marinelli

brings you her new romance

HEART OF THE DESERT

One searing kiss is all it takes for Georgie to know
Sheikh Prince Ibrahim is trouble....

But, trapped in the swirling sands, Georgie finally
surrenders to the brooding rebel prince—yet the
law of his land decrees that she can never
really be his....

Available October 2011.

Available only from Harlequin Presents®.